This Was The Reason Why He Didn't Want Women In The Shop. Too Distracting.

When Billy managed to step away from Jenny, he saw that she'd tucked her lower lip under her teeth with enough pressure that the flesh was bleaching white. What had been, up to that moment, a mere irritating attraction shifted right over to desire.

He wanted the pretty little schoolteacher in a way that had nothing to do with civility. He wanted to kiss the color back into her lip, to find out how hard she was capable of biting.

Then she looked up at him through thick lashes, and he saw his own desire mirrored in her eyes. She wasn't scared of him, nor was she mad at him.

As difficult as it was to believe, she wanted him, too.

* * *

Bringing Home the Bachelor is part of The Bolton Brothers trilogy: They live fast, ride hard and love fiercely!

* * *

If you're on Twitter, tell us what you think of Harlequin Desire! #harlequindesire

D0831329

Dear Reader,

Welcome back to Crazy Horse Choppers, the family business run by The Bolton Brothers: Billy (the creative one), Ben (the numbers guy) and Bobby (the salesman). They live fast, ride hard and love fiercely.

Billy Bolton doesn't like his life very much right now. After a wild youth that included jail time, he'd settled down into the life of a workaholic—he eats, breathes and lives building bikes. His dedication has paid off—the family company is becoming the name in custom-built motorcycles.

But success came with a price—in this case, his little brother Bobby filming him for "webisodes." Now Billy is semifamous, which is a real pain. Worse, his brother Ben arranged for him to build a bike for his wife, Josey's, school and Bobby's going to film him the whole time.

Billy knows he really shouldn't be around students— he's grumpy, he cusses, he's got too many tattoos, he occasionally throws things. And kids make him nervous. But then he meets Jenny Wawasuck, a teacher at the school—and a single mother to a teenager. Something about the petite woman grabs hold of Billy's attention and refuses to let go.

Billy knows he's not the kind of man any sane woman would be interested in. But Jenny's not afraid of him, and he finds himself doing something he never thought he'd do—chasing a woman.

Bringing Home the Bachelor is a sensual story about becoming the person you were always meant to be. It's also my twist on cowboys and Indians—bikers and Indians! I hope you enjoy reading it as much as I enjoyed writing it! Be sure to stop by www.sarahmanderson.com and join me for the latest on The Bolton Brothers!

Sarah

BRINGING HOME THE BACHELOR

—

SARAH M. ANDERSON

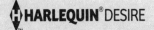

Recycling programs
for this product may
not exist in your area.

ISBN-13: 978-0-373-73267-8

BRINGING HOME THE BACHELOR

Copyright © 2013 by Sarah M. Anderson

Printed in U.S.A.

Books by Sarah M. Anderson

Harlequin Desire

A Man of His Word #2130
A Man of Privilege #2171
A Man of Distinction #2184
A Real Cowboy #2211
Straddling the Line #2232
Bringing Home the Bachelor #2254

*The Bolton Brothers

Other titles by this author available in ebook format.

SARAH M. ANDERSON

Award-winning author Sarah M. Anderson may live east of the Mississippi River, but her heart lies out West on the Great Plains. With a lifelong love of horses and two history teachers for parents, she had plenty of encouragement to learn everything she could about the tribes of the Great Plains.

When she started writing, it wasn't long before her characters found themselves out in South Dakota among the Lakota Sioux. She loves to put people from two different worlds into new situations and to see how their backgrounds and cultures take them someplace they never thought they'd go.

One of Sarah's books, *A Man of Privilege,* won the *RT Book Reviews* 2013 Reviewers' Choice Best Book Awards Series: Desire.

When not helping out at her son's school or walking her rescue dogs, Sarah spends her days having conversations with imaginary cowboys and American Indians, all of which is surprisingly well-tolerated by her wonderful husband. Readers can find out more about Sarah's love of cowboys and Indians at www.sarahmanderson.com.

To Mary, the most responsible oldest sibling
I've ever met! You've been with me
for every step of the way and
I truly couldn't do it without you.
We may not be sisters, but we're friends
and for that I'm forever grateful.

One

In the middle of the argument—the same argument Jenny had with her teenage son every morning—she found herself lost in a daydream. Just once, she wanted someone to take care of her. Just once, she wanted to feel pampered. *Just once,* she thought with a sigh, she wanted to know what it was like to have the world at her feet, instead of having everyone walk all over her.

"Why can't I go with Tige after school?" her son, Seth, whined from the passenger seat. Not that a fourteen-year-old boy would cop to whining. "He got a new motorcycle, said I could ride it. Better than wasting time waiting on you to get done with your stupid meeting."

"No motorcycles," Jenny said in the tone she used for attempting to reason with her first and second graders when her patience was thin. Hopefully, she and Seth would make it to school before she lost her temper. Only a few miles to go. She drove faster.

"Why not? Josey rides hers all over the place, and you know she wouldn't do it if it wasn't safe."

"Josey is a grown woman," Jenny said through gritted teeth. This was the difference between fourteen-year-old

Seth and eight-year-old Seth. The boy had always been able to tell when he shouldn't press his luck. "Josey's husband taught her how to ride, she's never had an accident, and you know good and well that she hasn't been on a bike since she got pregnant." Seth shuddered in immature horror. "May I remind you that Tige is a seventeen-year-old boy who drives too fast, doesn't own a helmet and has already crashed his bike twice? *No. Motorcycles.*"

"Aw, Mom. You're not being fair."

"Life isn't fair. Get used to it." Seth rolled his eyes so hard she heard it in the dark.

"If my dad were still here, he'd let me ride."

Before she could come up with a coherent response to Seth's newest favorite guilt trip, she rounded the last curve before the Pine Ridge Charter School, where she taught two grades in one classroom. Trucks and cars were parked everywhere, with massive, stadium-style lights ripping through the soft dawn light.

Shoot, Jenny thought as Seth leaned forward to stare at the three-ring circus. The battle with Seth had made her forget that today was the first day of filming at the school.

The Pine Ridge Charter School was the only school for grades one through eight within a two-hour drive. The school had been funded and built by her cousin Josey White Plume and her aunt, Sandra White Plume. They'd finished it before the first day of school last fall, mostly thanks to the donations of Crazy Horse Choppers, which was run by Ben Bolton and his brothers, Billy and Bobby. The Bolton boys made money hand over fist with their high-end, *very* expensive motorcycles. Josey had wound up marrying Ben Bolton—and was now pregnant with their first baby.

If that were all there was to it, it would be weird enough. But the crazy didn't stop there. Oh, no. Bobby Bolton had been filming "webisodes"—which Jenny didn't even think was a real word—of Billy Bolton building motorcycles at the Crazy Horse shop and posting the videos on the internet. Apparently, they were getting hundreds of thousands of hits, mostly because Billy cussed like a drunken sailor and occasionally threw tools at people. Jenny didn't have an internet connection, so she hadn't seen the show herself. She didn't want to. It sounded like entertainment aimed at the lowest common denominator.

But now the whole production had moved to her school. Billy Bolton was supposed to build a bike on site, teach the students how to use the tools and then the Boltons were going to auction the bike off and give the proceeds to the school. Bobby was going to film the whole thing.

Jenny didn't know which part of this plan she liked the least. Ben wasn't so bad. He was focused, intense and looked good on a bike, but he was a little too elite for Jenny's taste. He made Josey happy, though, so that made Jenny happy.

Bobby, the youngest of the Bolton brothers, talked to her only when he wanted something. He was handsome and charming and fabulously rich and she supposed that was more than enough for most women, but she didn't trust him.

She trusted Billy, the oldest, even less. He was—well, she didn't know if he was an actual Hell's Angel, but she wouldn't have been the least bit surprised to know he was in some sort of semicriminal biker gang. He was a massive man who everyone seemed mildly-to-severely afraid of. When she'd been introduced to him at Josey's wedding, he'd given off a vibe that had been something between quiet, dangerous and sexy. The combination had been thrilling—or would have been if she'd let herself be thrilled. He'd been a sight to behold, with his brown hair pulled back into a ponytail, a neatly trimmed beard and a tuxedo that fit him like a glove.

Like the other two Bolton brothers, Billy was gorgeous in his rough way and richer than sin—but of the three of them, he had waved his wealth around the least. Ben wasn't showy, but everything he owned was the best. Bobby let everyone know how rich and popular he was. But Billy? It was almost as if the family money pissed him off. Jenny had been struck mute by the way he'd glared down at her. She'd barely been able to squeak out a "pleased to meet you."

And now that man was going to have the run of *her* school and interact with *her* students.

It was one thing for that man to make her nervous while she was wearing a frilly dress at a wedding that cost more than her house and car put together. It was a whole different thing if that man looked at one of her students with that glare. She would not tolerate a whiff of improper, indecent or dangerous behavior from any Bolton, no matter how muscled he was. One step out of line, and Billy Bolton would find out exactly what kind of woman she was.

She pulled into her regular parking spot, and Seth was already out the door, gawking as a small group of people scurried around. Jenny was usually the first person at the school. She liked easing into the morning before a bunch of six-, seven- and eight-year-olds descended on her classroom. She made some tea, made sure she had all of her supplies ready and got herself mentally prepared for the day. And since Seth usually hung out in the multipurpose room practicing guitar, it was as close to Zen as Jenny got.

But today? No Zen for her. Instead, a woman yelled, "We have a problem—car in the shot," into a walkie-talkie as she brushed past Jenny while a man adjusted the lights—and managed to blind her with the beam.

Before she could shade her eyes, a figure spoke from beside her. "Jennifer? Hi, Bobby Bolton. We met at the wedding. Great to see you again. So glad to be out here, doing something good for the school. You do good work out here, and we're thrilled to be a part of it, but we're going to need you to move your car."

Jennifer. The hackles went up on the back of Jenny's neck. Yes, he'd been trying to compliment her, but her name was not Jennifer. It never had been. She had the legal documents to prove it. She was Jenny Marie Wawasuck.

She swung around slowly—slow enough that she heard Seth make a noise that sounded like *snerk*. Even a teenaged boy knew better than to call her *Jennifer.*

"Excuse me?" was the most polite thing Jenny could come up with.

Bobby had on a headset, and despite looking like the kind of guy who rarely got up before noon, he was as good-looking as ever. "As I'm sure you know, Jennifer, we're doing the shoot this morning. We're going to need you to move your car."

It was awfully early to have her last nerve snap, but it did. "Why?"

Bobby gave her the kind of smile that made her want to punch him in the stomach. "We're setting up a shot of Billy riding in, and we need the space." Bobby's voice was less complimentary now, more a direct order. "Move your car."

Of all the arrogant…Jenny paused—a trick she'd learned long ago worked on children of all ages to command attention. She drew herself up to her full height of five foot five inches, but she was still a good eight inches shorter than Bobby. She hated craning her neck, but she didn't have a stepstool handy.

"No. This is my spot. I always park here." Part of her knew she was being a tad irrational—it's not like moving the car was a huge deal—but she didn't want Bobby Bolton to think he could steamroll her whenever he felt like it.

Too often, too many people thought they could flatten her. They thought she wouldn't put up a fight because she was a nice girl or because she taught little kids or because she had nothing—especially that. Nothing but a parking spot.

Bobby's smile disappeared and he suddenly looked tired. "I know this is your spot, but I'd think a grown woman could handle parking somewhere else for one day. Thanks so much. Vicky?" he said into his headset. "Can we get Jennifer some coffee? Thanks." He turned his gaze back to her, and his fake-happy smile was back. "I know it's early, but once you move your car and have your coffee, I'm sure you'll feel better, Jennifer."

Jenny bristled under his patronizing tone, but before she could tell him that she didn't drink coffee, much less restate her position about not moving her darned car, a shadow loomed behind her, blocking out the spotlight.

A shiver raced up her arms and across her neck as a deep, powerful voice said, "Her name isn't Jennifer." As if to emphasize this point, a massive fist swung out from the shadows and hit Bobby in the arm so hard that he had to take a few steps back to keep his balance. "It's Jenny. Stop being a jerk."

Jenny swallowed as Billy Bolton brushed past her and stood next to his brother. She was not afraid of this man, she reminded herself. So what if he was a foot taller than she was, wearing really expensive-looking leather chaps over a pair of jeans and a tight-fitting black T-shirt that didn't look like the kind that cost seven dollars at Walmart? So what if he had on sunglasses and the sun hadn't even broken through the horizon? So what if he looked like some sort of bad-biker-boy fantasy come true?

He was on her territory, by God. She would not cower, and that was *that*.

So she squared her shoulders, put on her don't-mess-with-me glare and stood her ground. Then she realized what Billy had said.

He knew her name.

Weird goose bumps spread from her neck down her back. She would have been willing to bet that he wouldn't have been able to pick her out of a lineup, but here he was, punching Bobby because he'd called her the wrong name.

My school, my rez, she repeated to herself as she cleared her throat. "Right. Well, have fun making your little movie, gentlemen." She turned to walk into the building at a slow, deliberate pace, but Bobby circled around.

"We haven't solved our problem."

"Problem?" Billy asked. Jenny felt his voice rumble through her. She remembered now that he'd invoked that same sort of physical response in her the other time they'd met, too.

"Jennif—Jenny's car is in the shot." Bobby quickly corrected himself before Billy took another swing at him. "We need to get you on the bike riding up to the school with the sunrise, and her car will be in the way. I've asked her to move it—for the day," he added, giving her another sexy smile, "but because it's early and she hasn't had her coffee, she hasn't yet seen the value of temporarily relocating her vehicle."

What a load of hooey dressed up in double-talk. Did he think he could confuse her with a bunch of fancy language and the kind of smile that probably melted the average woman?

"Just because Josey gave you permission to film at this school does not mean I'm going to let you and your 'crew' disrupt my students' educations," she said through a forced smile.

Then something strange happened. Billy looked at her, leaned forward, took a deep breath—and appeared to be savoring it. "She doesn't drink coffee," he said as the woman Jenny had seen earlier walked up with a steaming mug of the stuff.

Okay, Billy Bolton was officially freaking her out. Jenny had been more or less invisible to the male race for—well, how old was Seth? Fourteen? Yes, fourteen years. No one wanted to mess with a single mother, and a mostly broke Indian one at that.

But Billy? He was not just paying attention to her name, or what she smelled like. He was paying attention to *her*. She had no idea if she should be flattered or terrified.

"You're not going to move your car?" he asked.

"No."

She couldn't see his eyes behind his glasses, but she got the feeling he was giving her the once-over. Then, with a curt nod, he turned around, walked to the front bumper of her car and picked up the whole dang thing. With his bare hands. True, it was a crappy little compact car that was about twenty years old, but still—he picked it up as if it didn't weigh much more than a laundry basket. If she wasn't so mad right now, she'd be tempted to do something ridiculous, like swoon at the sight of all his muscles in action. He was like every bad-boy fantasy she'd ever had rolled into one body.

"Hey—*hey!*" Jenny yelled as he rolled her car about thirty feet away and dropped it in the grass with a thud. "What the heck do you think you're doing?"

"Solving a problem." Billy dusted his hands off on his chaps and turned to face her, as if he regularly moved vehicles with his bare hands. "You."

That absolutely, totally *did it*. It was bad enough she had to take a constant stream of attitude from her son. She'd tried being nice and polite—like the good girl she was—but what had that gotten her? Nothing but grief.

"You listen to me, you—you—*you*." Before she knew what she was doing, she'd reached out and shoved—actually shoved—Billy Bolton.

Not that he moved or anything. Pushing his chest was

like pushing against a solid wall of stone. And all those stupid goose bumps set off again. She ignored them.

"I am not here for you or your brother or his film crew to treat like garbage. I am a teacher. This is my school. Got that?"

She thought she saw Billy's mouth curve up into something that might have been a grin. Was he laughing at her?

She reached up to shove him again—not that it would hurt him, but she had this irrational thought that something physical might be the only thing a man like him understood.

This time, Billy captured her hand with his massive fingers and held it. In an instant, all those goose bumps were erased by a licking flame of heat that ran roughshod over her body.

With effort, she held on to her anger and wrenched her hand away from his. "You listen to me—I don't care how big or scary or rich or famous you are—you're at my school, on my rez, mister. You make one mistake—touch one student, say something inappropriate—I'll personally grind you up into hamburger and feed you to the coyotes. Do I make myself clear?"

Billy didn't say a thing. He looked at her from behind his dark shades. The only reaction she could see was the possible curve of his lips behind his beard, but she couldn't even be sure about that.

"Mom," Seth said from behind her.

"We need to get filming, Jenny," Bobby added. He stepped between her and Billy and tried to herd her away.

She leaned around Bobby and leveled her meanest glare at Billy. "We aren't done here." Then she turned around and stomped off.

As she went, she swore she heard Billy say behind her, "No, I don't think we are."

Two

Billy stood there, thinking that his day had taken a turn for the better.

Had that pretty little cousin of Josey's really threatened to feed him to the coyotes? Man, no one threatened him anymore—except for his brothers. Everyone else either knew about his Wild Bill reputation—even though all that stuff had happened more than ten years ago—or they knew he had enough money to sue them back into the Dark Ages.

Hell, the pretty little woman named Jenny probably knew both of those facts—and she had threatened him anyway. He ran his fingers over the spot on his chest where she'd amusingly tried to shove him—right where he had a rose wrapped in thorns tattooed. He could still feel the warmth from her touch. How long had it been since a woman had touched him?

He'd always had terrible taste in women. He had the scars to prove it. He'd had other offers since the biker babes who used to hit on him—high-class women who were more interested in his newly made money than him. But Billy wasn't interested in having his heart ripped out again. And he usually threw off enough stay-away vibes to scare most women away.

In fact, if memory served, he had been sure that Jenny Wawasuck had been afraid of him when they'd met at Ben and Josey's wedding. He supposed he hadn't helped put her at ease.

Josey had asked him to wear a tux to her wedding in such a sweet way that he'd dug deep into his closet to find the one he'd had custom-made a few years ago when Bobby had insisted on dragging him to some sort of posh party in Hollywood. Even though it was his own suit, and fit well, the bow tie hadn't done anything to improve his mood. Seeing how happy his brother had looked getting married had been just another reminder of what Billy didn't have.

Jenny had been this cute little thing—nothing like the kind of woman he'd taken home back when he'd hit the bars as Wild Bill. And nothing like the vacuous, high-maintenance women he'd run into when Bobby forced him into those high-society parties. Her long hair had been curled but not teased, and her bare shoulders had been free of any kind of ink. She'd looked beautiful that day. She'd obviously been the kind of sweet, good-natured woman who avoided the likes of him. And the fact that he hadn't come up with a single decent thing to say to her?

Damn. The memory still made him burn.

Of course, she wasn't his type—and her type never went for guys like him. Easier to let it go at that.

Now, he turned to Bobby and let his brother shoo him onto his bike and instruct him to drive up and down the gravel road to school until the film crew told him to stop. Bobby had this irritating habit of wanting twenty takes for every ten seconds of footage. Normally, it drove Billy nuts, but today he was glad to have the chance to think.

He did his best thinking on his bikes. Usually, that meant solving the latest design problem or figuring out how to work around his dad or brothers. But today, riding up and down the same mile of territory that hardly qualified as a road, the problem he found himself thinking about was Jenny.

She'd smelled of baby powder, a soft scent that matched the woman he'd met at the wedding but seemed out of place on the woman who'd threatened him. Not a hint of coffee, and he knew Josey preferred tea when she was on the rez. The guess hadn't been a huge leap, but the way Jenny's eyes had widened when he'd been right? Worth it.

He still couldn't get over how she'd promised it wasn't over. Maybe he was getting soft in his thirties, but he found himself hoping she was right.

Finally, after an hour of rolling up and down the same mile, Bobby decided they had the footage he wanted. By that time, the school was overflowing. All the kids were there, and a fair number of their parents had come to watch, too.

Back when he'd earned his reputation the hard way, people had been in awe of him. Some had wanted to be on his good side, some had tried to prove they were bigger or badder. People's reactions had only gotten worse since this whole webisode thing started. People were watching him, expecting him to be funny or crude or what, he didn't know. All he knew was they were here for Wild Bill Bolton. And he hated it.

His brother Ben's wife, Josey, came up to him as he parked his bike next to the shop where they were going to be building the bike. "Morning, Billy," she said. "Everything go okay so far?"

Right. No doubt Jenny had had a little powwow with her cousin. "Bobby's still an ass—"

"Language! There are children present!"

It was going to be such a long day. "Twit. Bobby's still a twit."

Josey sighed. "Billy, remember the rules."

"Yeah, yeah, I know—language, attitude, no throwing things."

Josey patted him on the arm. "It's just three weeks."

Sure, it was only three weeks at the school, but he was stuck with Bobby running his life for the foreseeable future. He'd only agreed to do this show because Ben said this was a good way to justify the cost of new equipment for the shop, and Billy loved new equipment. Hell, testing out a new tool was half the fun of building a bike. Plus, he'd thought it was a good way to keep the peace in the family. Now he wasn't so sure.

Sure, Billy guessed it was nice that people recognized him now, and yeah, it was probably good for his ego that someone had started a Facebook page called The Wild Bill Bolton Fan Club. But most of him wanted "Real American Bikers," which was what Bobby called the webisodes, to fail and fail big. That way, he could go back to doing what he did best—building custom motorcycles. No more cameras, no more groupies, no more being famous.

Back to building his bikes in peace and quiet.

Although that didn't look like it was going to happen anytime soon. "Real American Bikers" was getting a healthy number of hits on YouTube, where Bobby was hosting a channel for it—whatever the hell that meant. Billy hadn't actually watched more than about two minutes of the show. It was too painful. Too much of a reminder that he could never really leave his Wild Bill reputation behind him.

"Oh, here comes Don Two Eagles," Josey was saying as she waved an older guy over. "Don, this is—"

"Billy Bolton. You look like your old man," Don said. Didn't sound like a compliment, and Billy sure as hell didn't take it as one.

Ben had told Billy all about Don. "You're the guy who broke Dad's jaw back at Sturgis in the eighties, right?"

"Damn straight," Don said.

"Language!" Josey snipped as she checked to see if any kids had been listening.

"I put your old man down, and I ain't afraid to do the same to you, so you best behave, hear?"

"Don," Josey said under her breath. Billy got the feeling that this was a conversation they'd had before. Then she turned on the charm. "Now, the kids are going to come out and line up. Bobby thinks it'll be a nice shot if we introduce some of the older students to you personally and you shake their hands, so we'll start filing them past you. Can you handle that?"

"Yes."

"I'll be watching you," Don said before being called away by the production crew.

"Heavens, can you believe Bobby actually wants to bring your father out here and let him and Don go at it?" Josey's voice dropped down to a whisper. "Sometimes I don't know about that brother of yours."

"Makes two of us."

This was why he liked Josey. She understood how the Bolton family worked and was committed to keeping it from imploding. Ben had picked well.

Then he heard himself ask, "Will Jenny be bringing her class out?"

Josey gave him an odd look. "No, the first and second graders aren't allowed in the shop."

"I wasn't trying to break her car," he added.

"I know. Just solving a problem. That's what you do best, Billy." She patted him on the arm again—she had that whole mothering thing down.

Billy was about to rub the dust off his tires when Vicky,

the production assistant, came up to him. "We need to get you miked, Billy."

Vicky definitely fell into the category of women who were afraid of him. Her production company, Villainy Productions, sounded far tougher than she was. Miking Billy usually involved taping a mike to Billy's chest, and she didn't seem to think his tattoos were impressive.

"Well," she said, surveying the fitted T-shirt Billy wore. "I guess…you're going to have to take the shirt off?"

Billy grabbed the hem of his T-shirt, but before he could peel it off, the doors to the school burst open and about fifty kids came pouring out. Almost immediately, Josey was next to him, a hand on his arm. "Can we do this somewhere else?"

Vicky swallowed. She worked real hard on not being alone with him. Which was funny—Bobby was the much bigger threat to the female race. Billy hadn't even been with a woman in…

Damn. That turned into a depressing train of thought. The fact was, it'd been a long time since he'd gotten tired of going home with the kind of woman who looked like she was auditioning for a heavy-metal music video and waking up alone. Years.

Since then, he'd thrown himself into building bikes. Which wasn't such a bad thing—it kept him out of trouble. He was good at it, which had made him a boatload of money—also not a bad thing. However, with the money had come a different kind of woman—older, richer, more mercenary, if that were possible. Billy had no interest in those women. None. The one time he'd dated a woman out of his league, he'd gotten his heart run over like roadkill. It was easier just to build more bikes.

But now building bikes was making him famous. Hell, half the time he was afraid to leave his house in the morning. A few groupies had showed up at the Crazy Horse shop and tried to treat him like a rock star, screaming and even throwing a pair of panties. Which Bobby had filmed—if he hadn't set the whole thing up in the first place. No way, no how was Billy falling into that trap. He'd rather be alone than be with a woman who was only interested in using him.

Which meant he was alone.

"Go around the side of the school. We can't have him stripping out here in front of the students," Josey said before hurrying over to help explain the rules to the kids.

Not that it was stripping, but yeah, even he saw the wrong in taking off his shirt in front of kids. He had tattoos—lots of them. The kind that scared small children and little old ladies.

So he trudged around to the side of the building with Vicky following at a safe distance and whipped off his shirt. Vicky clipped the battery pack to his jeans, ducked under his upraised arm, and handed him the mike while she ripped off a piece of medical tape. They'd learned after the first show that clipping the mike to the collar of Billy's shirt didn't work—too much static from the machines ruined the audio feed. Now they taped the mike to his chest and let the shirt filter out the extra noise.

Vicky handed him the tape, and he put the mike on above the rose and thorns—above where Jenny had touched him.

As the thought of the sassy little teacher crossed his mind again, his ears developed a weird burning sensation, as if someone were talking about him. He glanced around and saw that—much to his chagrin—an entire class of undersized tykes was crowded around the windows, staring at him.

And behind them stood a shocked Jenny Wawasuck.

Her eyes were as wide as hubcaps and her mouth had

dropped open as she looked at his exposed torso. Billy froze—he was pretty sure this violated someone's rule.

If he were Ben, he would probably figure out some calm, cool way to exit the situation and mitigate the damage. If he were Bobby, he would flex and pose for the pretty little teacher. He wasn't either of them. And as such, he had no idea what to do besides brazen it out. So he stood there and stared back at her, almost daring her to come out and turn him into coyote food.

She said something sharply to the kids, who all scrambled back from the windows as if she'd poked them with a cattle prod. Then she shot him the meanest look he'd ever seen a woman give him—which was saying something—then pulled the blinds.

The whole thing took less than a minute.

Damn. He was screwed. The only question was, how badly? Would she kick him off this rez? Would Don Two Eagles do the kicking?

He sighed. This was how things went. He wasn't trying to stir up trouble, but it always found him anyway. All he could do now—since he'd promised to watch his language and not throw things—was wait for Jenny to storm out of the building and tear him a new one.

It'd be easier if it were Don. Billy knew men like Don, knew how they thought, knew what to expect. But a woman like Jenny was something else, someone he didn't know and couldn't anticipate. A sweet little first-grade teacher—with one hell of an edge to her.

Given the way his thoughts kept turning back to when she'd touched him this morning, he was going to be spending a lot more time trying to anticipate her.

Resigned to his fate, Billy slid his shirt back on and went out to his assigned position. He'd never understood why he had to be the one on camera—other than the fact that he was the one who built the bikes. Ben didn't have to be on camera at all. Bobby was the one who had the Hollywood thing going on, from the way he wore a tie every day to the way he talked circles around everyone. Times like this, Billy wished he could be as smooth as Bobby. The man was good with people—well, people who weren't Jenny Wawasuck.

Billy stood there, keeping an eye on the door as the smaller kids were introduced to him in a group. Where was Jenny? Surely she wouldn't let such an offensive act as taking off his shirt in front of a bunch of first and second graders pass. Flashing a lifetime of ink at a bunch of little kids didn't seem like something Jenny Wawasuck would let stand.

As he started shaking the hands of the bigger kids, the ones who'd be "helping" him build the bike for charity, Billy realized two things. One, Jenny wasn't going to come out and pick another fight with him, and two—he was disappointed.

One of the kids shook his hand and said, "Hi again, Mr. Bolton." Billy's attention snapped back to the present.

The kid looked familiar. Billy didn't have a head for names and faces, but he knew he'd met him before. "I know you, right?"

"We met at Josey's wedding," the boy said with a stammer. "I was an usher."

"Yeah." Billy shook his hand again. Probably some sort of nephew or cousin or something. "See you in the shop."

The kid's face brightened up. He couldn't be much more than thirteen. Billy remembered being that age once—although he tried not to think about it too much.

He got to the end of the line and mercifully, Bobby didn't make them do the whole meet-and-greet thing all over again. Don and Josey began herding the kids into the shop to set up the next shot—Billy explaining how the kids were going to help him—when it happened.

The back door of the school swung open and out stepped Jenny. Billy's temperature spiked, which didn't make a damn bit of sense. Now that he could see her in the full light of the morning, he noticed she had her long hair pulled back into a boring bun-thing at the base of her neck. She wore a white-collared shirt under a pale blue cardigan, all of which was over an exceptionally plain khaki skirt. The whole effect was of someone trying not to be noticed.

Billy noticed her anyway, his heart rate picking up an extra few RPMs. She shouldn't look sexy to him—but she did. Underneath that schoolmarm appearance was a hot-blooded woman with a smart mouth who wasn't afraid of him. The combination was heady.

She stood on the steps, hands on hips that couldn't be hidden by her boring skirt, and glared at him. Normally, Billy would either stare her down—he did that all the time—or turn away and pretend he hadn't seen the disapproval in her eyes.

Instead—and this was insane—he gave her a mock salute, just to make her mad all over again. He couldn't help himself. What had she thought of all the tattoos? Did they scare her, or had she liked them for the art they were?

"We need you inside," Bobby said, once again stepping between Billy and Jenny. Over Bobby's shoulder, Billy saw Jenny make a motion with her hands that perfectly conveyed both her disgust and also her fury before she turned and went back inside.

No, this wasn't over. Not by a long shot.

Three

Billy needed a drink.

Not that he drank much anymore, but still. A day of having to watch his temper around kids who kept picking up his tools and putting them down in the wrong places. A whole day of Bobby making him say the same thing over and over in different positions. A long day of *not* building a bike.

Better be a stiff drink.

It was almost over. The kids had, by and large, gone home. Only that one kid, the one he'd met at Josey's wedding, was still in the shop. Billy had been allowed to take his mike off, and while Bobby and his production crew were still doing things, none of them required Billy to smile for a camera.

What was that kid's name? Billy thought hard, but he drew a blank. "You're still here."

"Yeah, my mom stays late to talk with the pregnant girls."

Suddenly, the feeling that Billy should remember this kid's name got a lot stronger. "Yeah?"

"Yeah." The boy looked at his feet and scuffed his toe

on the floor. "I'm sorry about the way she blew up at you this morning. She gets like that sometimes."

Wait—wait a damn minute. Was this kid saying that Jenny was his *mom?*

No way—not possible. This kid was a teenager. Jenny couldn't be that old.

Unless...unless she'd been young. The familiar guilt tried to kick open the heavy steel door Billy kept it trapped behind. This kid could only be Jenny's son if she'd been a teenager. And she'd kept him.

Damn. Fate had a freakin' funny sense of humor sometimes.

The next question had to be whether or not she was married, because there was no way in hell that Billy was going to keep entertaining thoughts of a married woman. Bolton men were loyal for life. Whatever problems they might have as a family—and Lord knew there were a lot of them—they respected the family, which meant they respected other families, too.

"So where's your dad?" That probably wasn't the best way to ask the question, but Billy had never been known for his tact.

The kid shrugged. "Dunno. Gone before I was born, I guess. Mom says we're better off without him, anyway."

Two thoughts crossed his mind quick. First, Jenny was available, so he could keep right on thinking about how she looked at him with that passion—okay, passionate fury—in her eyes. Second, though, was that a boy needed a man in his life. Especially a boy on the verge of becoming a man.

"You kids aren't really going to help me build the bike, you know."

As if to illustrate this point, Vicky called over, "Okay, wave at the camera, Billy."

Feeling stupid, Billy waved to the camera that had been installed overhead. He was going to work nights and weekends to build the bike himself, hours of which would be compressed into two- to four-minute segments on the show. The rest would be staged shots with kids.

The rest of the crew went out to the truck, probably to review the footage. Bobby liked to check the tapes. Although Billy would never admit this to the little twit, he thought Bobby was impressively focused on making the show as good as it could be.

"Yeah, I know." The boy sounded positively depressed. Then he perked up. "I can still help. Mom always stays late for her after-school program, so I'm here a lot."

Billy worked alone. Even in his shop, he did his own thing while his guys did the assembly stuff. But something about this boy—and his mother—kept his mouth shut.

Billy wasn't looking to be a father. That ship had sailed seventeen years ago, and it wasn't going to make a return voyage. But a shop teacher could still make a big difference. Billy's shop teacher in high school, Cal Horton, had saved Billy's life on at least three occasions and kept him out of prison twice, which was more than his own father, Bruce Bolton, had ever done.

Yeah, he didn't have to be this kid's father. But Cal would expect him to pay it forward.

"You want to help?" The kid nodded eagerly, his eyes bright. "I could use an assistant. Find a broom and sweep up this place. It's a wreck, and a good shop is a clean shop. Keeps dust and junk from getting into the parts."

He thought the kid was going to balk at manual labor. Billy didn't nag. He went back to organizing his tools and waited for the kid to make up his mind.

Less than forty seconds later, the boy was sweeping.

Billy smiled to himself. "You do a good job and keep at it, maybe we'll get you on a bike."

"Really?" The kid grinned. Then it faded. "My mom won't like that."

Yeah, he knew that, too. His own mother had never been a fan of some of the things Billy did. Most of them, actually.

"Aw, hell. What your mom doesn't know won't hurt her."

"You don't know my mom very well." The boy kept sweeping. A moment later, he added, "I got a friend who's got a bike, but she won't let me near it. Says she doesn't want me to get hurt." He made a noise that sounded like teenager-speak for "can you believe that?" "It's not as cool a bike as yours, though."

Maybe half of Billy's childhood had been spent on the back of a bike, often directly against his mother's stated wishes. His father had loved his mother dearly, but they rarely saw eye to eye on basic parenting questions, such as which activities were fun versus life-threatening. And Billy had survived just fine.

Well, mostly fine.

"I'll make a deal with you. You keep your grades up and help me out in the shop, I'll get you on a bike." He leveled a finger at the huge smile on the kid's face. "*But* you do what I say, when I say it, no questions asked. I don't need some pissant kid jerking around my shop. I'll throw your ass out of here the moment you screw up. Got it?"

The sudden gasp that came from the doorway told him that someone had screwed up, all right.

Him.

Jenny waved goodbye to the last of the girls from her Teen and Parents—TAPS—meeting and checked the multipurpose room for Seth. Seth hated the TAPS meetings and put as much distance as possible between him and the pregnant girls—most of whom he'd grown up playing with. Jenny supposed she should be thrilled that Seth hadn't hit the age where he thought of girls in a sexual way, but would it have killed the boy to have a bit of compassion? After all, Jenny had been one of those girls once.

Seth wasn't in the multipurpose room. The guitar was still in its case. Where was that boy?

Oh, no. The shop. Billy Bolton.

That man, Jenny thought as she ran down the hall. Yup, his bike was still parked in her spot. The door to the shop was open, and she heard voices inside. There was no missing Billy's deep rumble—she wasn't sure she could forget the way that voice hummed through her body. Even now, she got goose bumps. She also heard the softer voice of her son.

Oh, Lord, Seth was talking with Billy—and, from the tone of it, Billy was yelling at her boy. Running faster, the first words she caught were "...need some pissant kid jerking around my shop. I'll throw your ass out of here the moment you screw up. Got it?"

She gasped as she flew into the shop. "*What* did you say to my son?"

Seth jumped six inches off the floor, but Billy—sitting behind a table with a massive tool-thing in his hands—didn't even move. At least this time he wasn't wearing glasses. Jenny wasn't sure that helped, though, because now she could see the way his light brown eyes bore into her, like heat-seeking missiles.

No one else was in the building. She'd gotten here just in time. Billy stared at her, something that looked like contempt on his face. Seth looked six kinds of miserable all at once. God only knew what Billy had been saying to her baby boy to make him look like he was on the verge of crying.

She intended to find out, by God. She stalked over to the table and slammed her hands down on the top. The tools rattled and Seth warned, *"Mom,"* behind her, but she had had it with this man.

"I asked you a question, and don't you dare pull that silent crud on me. I heard you—I know you can talk. What do you think you're doing, speaking to my son using that kind of language?" When she didn't get an immediate response, she shouted back over her shoulder, "Seth, get your things."

"But, *Mom*," he whined again.

Then Billy stood up—all God-only-knew how many inches and pounds of him rose to his feet, slow and steady and not the least bit intimidated by her.

Jenny swallowed, refusing to allow herself to be intimidated by him, either. Even though he could pick her up and throw her over his shoulder like some big, gorgeous caveman, if he wanted to.

"Calm down."

Of all the nerve—was he actually going to try to talk his way out of this? "I will do no such thing. If I have my way, you won't be back on this reservation tomorrow. What is wrong with you? Stripping in front of a bunch of school children? Picking up my car? Threatening Seth? Are you insane?"

As she spoke, Billy walked around the table. He wasn't moving at tackling speeds, but his destination was unmistakable. She took one step backward, then another as Billy advanced on her.

"What are you doing?" she demanded.

Another step toward her. When he saw the effect he was having on her, one of his eyebrows notched up, which made him look almost amused. "Talking. To you." Another step. "You still sweeping?"

"What?"

It was only when Seth said, "Yes, sir," that she realized he hadn't been talking to her.

One more step.

"This is talking? You're trying to frighten me, but it

won't work," she said as he boxed her into a corner, an intense look on his face. She should be terrified—maybe she was—but that didn't explain the goose bumps that were all over her. Everything about her was tuned in to him—the way his muscles coiled and uncoiled with each step, the way he was…smiling? Was that possible?

Then, unexpectedly, Billy stopped while still a good four feet from her and looked over his shoulder. She was almost in a corner, but if she broke to the left fast enough, she could probably make it out the door. But if she did that, she'd leave Seth in here with this man, and she didn't want to do that.

This was a clear example of the devil you know versus the devil you don't. Except that in both cases, Billy Bolton was the devil.

When he faced her again, one corner of his mouth was unmistakably curved into a smile. "No, *this* is talking."

The sight of Billy Bolton grinning—at her—threw whatever Jenny had been planning to say right out the window.

Oh, my. Somewhere, underneath that beard and the dark glares was a *very* handsome man with surprisingly kind eyes. Her mind flashed back to the expanse of muscle she'd seen earlier that afternoon. Muscles and more muscles, covered in tattoos that should have scared the stuffing out of her, but all she'd thought of doing was tracing the lines on his skin and reading the story he'd written there.

Those vicious goose bumps ran rough all over her body, but this time, heat flashed behind them, leaving her skin quivering. Heck, her whole body quivered. Including parts of her that hadn't quivered in years.

"What are you going to do?" she asked, and was mortified to hear her voice come out somewhat lower and huskier than normal.

His eyes—a silky brown—darkened, and for a flash of

a second, his gaze darted down to her lips. Her body, acting of its own volition, responded by darting her tongue out and licking her lips.

It was like they were doing a dance, one with tiny, complex steps. The air sharpened between them, and she felt her head tip back. He responded by sucking in air, and she felt her body do the same thing. Two bodies moving in time together, creating a rhythm all their own.

It had been a long time since she'd danced. A long time since she'd *wanted* to dance.

And she wanted to dance with Billy Bolton, of all the wildly inappropriate people.

She had to get control of this situation before something terrible happened, like Billy pinning her to the wall, pressing all those muscles against her and kissing the heck out of her.

Yes. That would be terrible, indeed. Awful. Possibly the worst thing that could ever happen to her.

So why did she want so badly for him to do exactly that?

"Nothing you don't want me to."

And he stopped. No more steps toward her, no more hungry looks. No more dancing.

Jenny forced away all thoughts of her body moving in time with Billy's. They didn't go very far, just to the back of her mind, but far enough that she could think. "I will not have you threaten my son with such language." Her voice was still sultry. "Nor will I have you putting on such an indecent display in front of the children."

"Josey told me to go around the side of the school to get miked up so I wasn't in front of the other kids. I didn't know your classroom was there." Almost imperceptibly, he leaned in. The distance between them felt so sharp she thought it might cut her.

She could see Josey doing that. She'd assumed he'd been acting like his brother Bobby—showing off, making a scene—but she could see him trying to do the right thing. Maybe. "You were threatening Seth."

"With kicking him out of the shop if he doesn't pull his weight. Are you going to feed me to the coyotes for that?"

He tilted his head and looked her over again. Anytime she wanted to stop quivering would be great.

"You moved my car."

"You want me to move it back?" Then he flexed. It wasn't an exaggerated thing, but his chest and arms tightened under the shirt, then released.

Jenny's breath caught. Apparently, she'd lost her mind at some point in the past few minutes, because she wanted to tell him to do just that—but only if he took his shirt off.

"No."

"How old are you?"

Heat flooded her cheeks. "You can't ask me that."

Billy jerked his chin over his shoulder. "How old is he?"

Much more heat and she was going to start sweating. "That is none of your business!" And before she could stop herself, she asked, "How old are you?"

He didn't even hesitate. Men. "Thirty-four."

Five years older than she was.

"Mr. Bolton? I swept the floor."

The sound of Seth's voice snapped Jenny out of her man-induced insanity. "You what?"

"He swept up." Billy swung around and surveyed the shop. "Not bad, kid."

"He *what?*" Jenny looked at the now-clean shop floor. "Seth cleaned something? Because you threatened him?"

Billy looked back over his shoulder at her—only a quick glance, but Jenny felt the disapproval of his gaze. Then he walked around the shop, studying the floor. "Not bad at all," he said to Seth, and Jenny couldn't miss the way Seth's face lit up at the compliment.

What the heck? She and Seth fought over chores all the time, but Billy Bolton had him looking happy to clean?

When had she lost all control over the situation?

Oh, yeah—the moment she'd gotten out of her car this morning.

"So, did I do a good enough job? Can I help you in the morning?"

Jenny shook her head, trying to remember the last time she'd seen Seth look this excited about something.

"Depends on what your mother says."

That was the last thing she expected to come out of Billy's mouth.

"What?" That was how many *what*s in the past five minutes? She was starting to sound clueless—a feeling she hated.

Billy motioned toward the far corner of the shop. "You signed a release for him to appear on the show, but if he's going to be helping me out in the shop, he'll be filmed the whole time."

Jenny stepped forward and looked. She hadn't noticed the small camera with the red light before, but she saw it now. "What's that for?"

"They'll film me the whole time I'm building, then speed up the footage. If the kid helps, he'll be on film a lot more." He leaned to the side, and Jenny realized that they were less than two feet apart. "It's your call." Then Billy turned to Seth, "You've got to pull your weight. I hear that you're not helping your mom at home or your grades drop, you're out of here. I don't tolerate slackers."

Seth's gaze darted between her and Billy. Clearly, he was waiting for her to blow up like she had that morning. And she was still mad about the language Billy had used around her son.

The only thing was, she liked everything Billy had said. She couldn't believe that she was on the verge of agreeing to let Seth spend more time with Billy Bolton, but what could she do? Seth wasn't a little boy anymore, and something told her that he'd be safer with Billy than he would be if he were running around with Tige or any of his thuggish friends.

Billy turned and looked at her, one eyebrow raised in silent challenge.

"Can I, Mom? *Please?*"

This was a rock, and Billy Bolton was a hard place. The way his chest had *not* moved when she pushed it? A very hard place.

"We'll see how tomorrow goes."

"Was that a yes?" Seth hopped from foot to foot, a ball of nervous energy. "That was a yes, right? Yes!"

"Hey," Billy thundered. "Settle. Your mom told you to go get your things, so get moving."

Seth was gone before the broom hit the ground. She turned to Billy to lay down the law on the probationary day, but he beat her to the punch. "I won't make any promises about cussing—too set in my ways. I'd bet you dimes to dollars that he's heard it all, anyway. He's safer with me than he is with any of those hotshot troublemakers he calls friends."

Had Seth told him about Tige? Or was he that good at guessing?

He leaned in closer—less than a foot separated them now, and she thought he was going to kiss her. Different parts of her brain screamed out "No!" and "Yes!" at the same time, paralyzing her. She couldn't lean in, and she couldn't pull away.

But he didn't kiss her. Instead, he took another one of those savoring breaths. "Yeah, tea," he said in a low voice that set off another round of quivering she could only pray he didn't notice. "You should know something about me, Jenny. I keep my promises, or I don't make them."

The air stopped moving into or out of her lungs. Heck, everything stopped as he looked down into her eyes, so focused that she wasn't sure she'd ever move again.

"Mom? I got my stuff." Seth's head popped back into the room as Billy straightened up and put a respectable distance between the two of them. "I'll do my homework when I get home, okay? And you'll be here in the morning, right, Mr. Bolton? And I can help?" He sounded so excited that she wouldn't have been surprised to see him start spinning in circles like he used to do when he was four.

Seth eager to do his homework? A man flirting with her? Jenny looked around the shop, wondering if she'd woken up in an alternate dimension that morning.

Billy huffed as if he were insulted. "Mr. Bolton is my grandpa. My name is Billy."

"Yes, sir, Billy!" Then Seth spun and all-out ran for the car.

Billy turned back to her. She needed to say something fast—she couldn't let him dominate this interaction—or whatever it was. She was still in control of things, by God. But her brain was still muddled up, so the best thing she came up with was, "Are we done here?"

He smiled—a full-on, melt-in-her-mouth smile, the likes of which she had never seen before. "No," he said, moving toward his workbench. "We're not."

Four

Seth was up and dressed before Jenny's alarm clock went off. He rushed her through her oatmeal. They arrived at the school a good twenty minutes earlier than normal.

Billy was already there. Light shined through the shop's open door, despite the chill of the October morning. "Bye" was all she heard as Seth threw the door open. Then he was gone.

Jenny fought the urge to follow him. He wasn't a baby anymore, she kept reminding herself. And she had no desire to see Billy Bolton first thing in the morning.

Unfortunately, her mind took that image and threw some sheets and pillows into the mix, and suddenly, she had a *great* desire to see Billy first thing in the morning.

Just because Billy was treating her son well and paying attention to her didn't mean she should develop a crush on him. It didn't matter if he had a melt-in-her-mouth smile, more muscles than God and money to burn. He was still a hard-core biker with a foul mouth. Heaven only knew what he did for a good time, but Jenny was willing to bet that it was something she would not approve of.

So she went inside and reviewed her lesson plans. When

she was done, she still had half an hour before the students showed up.

She stood in front of her electric teakettle, at war with herself. Should she go out there and check on the shop? Or was that being too overbearing?

Oh, to heck with it. Just because Billy had said all those things about promises in that serious manner didn't mean he was honorable. Wanting to visit the shop had nothing to do with how he looked with or without his shirt on. Nothing at all.

She made two cups of tea and walked out to the shop. For some reason, her stomach was turning. What the heck did she have to be nervous about?

That question was answered the moment she set foot inside. Blinking through the bright lights, she saw that devastating smile on Billy's face.

Maybe she was dreaming, but if she didn't know any better, she'd say that smile was for her.

It wasn't possible. Men didn't look at her with interest—with need. Men looked at her shabby clothes and her rusty car and her smart-mouthed teenager and kept right on walking. If they looked at her at all.

Except for yesterday. And, as Billy rose from his stool and made his way over to her, possibly also today. Seth hadn't given her a lot of time to apply makeup this morning, which she barely wore anyway, but she was suddenly quite glad she'd managed to brush on a little blush and hit her lids with some eyeliner.

"That for me?" Billy asked, looking down at the mugs in her hands.

"Yes."

She offered a mug up to him. His hand was so large that there was no way to avoid touching him unless she threw the tea at him.

So she had to stand there and not react as his fingertips

skimmed over the backs of hers so lightly that she found herself shivering. The touch was much gentler than she would have given a man of his size credit for. Immediately, her mind took off in crazy directions, although she tried to slam the door on those thoughts. She was *not* lusting after, crushing on or, God forbid, even *liking* Billy Bolton.

Then the mug was in his hand and the contact was over. They stood there for a second, looking at each other. Had he felt the same shock she had? Of course not, she tried to tell herself. She was being as silly as the girls in her TAPS meetings, falling head over heels because of a grin and a touch. She had one job here, and that was to make sure Seth was doing okay. No attraction, no flirting. Just mothering.

"How's it going?"

Billy held her gaze for a beat longer. She could almost hear him reminding her they weren't done here, but instead he said, "Got him sorting out fasteners. They got all mixed up when we unloaded." He pointed with his chin to where Seth was sitting at a table, staring at a pile of nuts and bolts with a look of intense concentration on his face.

"I can't tell if this is a one-half or a nine-sixteenths." Jenny could hear the frustration in Seth's voice.

"Here, let me see—"

She had taken two steps when Billy grabbed her shoulder, holding her in place. He boomed, "Figure it out, kid. It ain't rocket science. You can't size a bolt, you can't build a bike."

She froze, waiting for the fit Seth would pitch. It didn't happen. Seth screwed up his face, scratched his head and then Jenny almost saw the lightbulb go on. He looked around, grabbed a wrench and started measuring.

"Good job," Billy said, and his hand squeezed Jenny's shoulder. Not tight, just a gentle pressure. It sent shock waves down her back that almost buckled her knees. He was so strong, but the sensation straddled the line between tender and erotic.

Then he let go, trailing his fingers down her arm. That—that was purely erotic. If she weren't so determined not to let this man have an impact on her, her knees would have given way.

"Thanks for the tea," he said, low and quiet as he walked past her.

She stood there, wondering what the heck she was supposed to do with *that*. Billy was flirting with her, she was sure of it. Pretty sure, anyway. She was so out of practice that even if she wanted to flirt back, she wouldn't know how. Maybe that was the problem.

Billy settled back onto his stool, his gaze on her. "See you later?"

Was she being dismissed? That didn't match with everything he'd just made her feel. Maybe she'd read him wrong.

"What?"

He shot her one of those intimidating glares, and for a second she *knew* she was being dismissed. But then he turned, pointedly looking over his shoulder—right at the small camera with the steady red light. Then he stared at her again, and she realized he'd asked her a question, not given her an order.

"I'll, uh, stop by after my meeting?"

"Yeah, okay, Mom," Seth said, clearly preoccupied. "Bye."

But Billy? He favored her with one of those half-hidden smiles that told her loud and clear that was the answer he was looking for.

He wanted to see her later.

Jenny all but floated back to her classroom.

Billy couldn't say how he knew that Jenny had walked into the shop. He sure as hell didn't see or hear her. He had his welding mask on and was holding down one end of a pipe as Seth tried his hand at cutting it with a miter saw. Don Two Eagles stood on the other side. Billy was watching Seth's hands; Don was watching Billy. He couldn't hear anything over the whine of metal against metal.

He knew Jenny had come in, all the same. And he didn't like it.

The shop—*any* shop—had always been a place apart from femininity. Josey didn't come to the shop very often, and when she did, she wasn't there very long. Even Cass, the receptionist at the Crazy Horse Choppers headquarters—who was as tough as a woman could be—stayed off the shop floor. Billy liked it that way. Nothing and no one to distract him from the choppers.

Except it didn't work like that here.

Seth finished cutting the pipe without also cutting off a finger or thumb. He even remembered to turn the blade off before doing anything else. Then he peeled off the welder's mask Billy had made him wear. "That was so awesome!"

Billy took his mask off, too. Damned if that woman wasn't sitting on his stool at his table, two cups of tea in front of her and a small smile on her face.

Double damned if he wasn't thrilled to see her there.

"How's it going?" Her gaze danced between the three men and their protective gear.

"Billy's letting me cut a pipe!" Seth grabbed the pipe and took it over to Jenny.

She regarded the rough, angular cut with suspicion. "How…nice, sweetie."

"Mom," Seth whined as Billy choked back a laugh.

"It's part of the frame," he explained, wondering if the tea was for him, the kid or Don.

Jenny's eyes got a little wide.

"What?" Billy asked, mentally slapping himself when it came out as defensive.

"You really are building this from scratch?"

"Women," Don muttered under his breath as he stripped off his shop apron and checked his watch. "Gotta get home. You guys going to be okay here?" He directed the question to Jenny, but he kept a wary eye on Billy.

For some reason, Billy thought about decking the old man. Who was he to suggest that Jenny and her kid weren't safe with Billy? He had been nothing but a gentleman so far. Except for the part where he'd moved her car. Oh, yeah, and stripped off his shirt. But other than that, he'd been a paragon of virtue.

"I'm not my old man," he muttered.

Don didn't back down. "It ain't a matter of if the apple falls from the tree. It's a matter of how far it fell."

The two men stared at each other.

"Don, we'll be fine." Jenny's voice was calm and surprisingly unconcerned with the standoff going on in front of her.

Don shot Billy a hell of a mean look, but said, "See you all tomorrow," and left.

Billy turned back to Jenny and Seth. The kid was holding his length of pipe against the plans, trying to figure out how to put a puzzle together with only one piece. Jenny, however, was still sitting on his stool, her lips hidden behind her cup of tea. She looked as if she were waiting for something. What, he didn't know.

This was why he didn't like women in the shop. The only expectations he was comfortable with were design specs and delivery dates, *not* rules of civility.

"He doesn't like you."

Seth snorted in amusement as he studied the design. "Yeah, but Don doesn't like any *wasicu*."

Jenny's eyes flew open as she slammed her cup back on the table. Tea sloshed everywhere. "Seth!"

"A what?"

The kid went red. "White...man," Jenny replied without meeting his gaze.

Yeah, right. Billy had been called enough names in his lifetime to know an insult when he heard one. He leveled one of his meaner looks at the kid, who physically shrank right before him. "Yeah, well, I'm not like any *whatever* he's ever met. Now suit up. We've got more pipe to cut."

Billy had never seen a kid move as fast as Seth did. Billy walked over to Jenny and held out a pair of earplugs. "Don't look at the saw without goggles," he told her as she stared at the plugs.

"It wasn't that loud when I came in. Do I really need these?"

If Billy had let her son get anywhere near a power tool without all the proper precautions, she'd probably have thrown a fit. But when it came to her own well-being?

She was the kind of woman who put herself last, he realized. Even when she didn't have to.

So he didn't bother telling her that the saw was always loudest at the beginning of the cut. Instead, he leaned forward, smoothed the few strands of hair that had come loose from her schoolmarm bun and tucked the plugs into her ears for her.

Her skin, from her cheeks to the back of her neck, flushed a beautiful pink as he pressed the plugs into place. Then, because he doubted that she wouldn't watch him and the kid work the saw, he snagged a pair of goggles from the table. He stretched the elastic back so that it wouldn't tangle on her hair and settled the plastic on the bridge of her nose. It wasn't his fault that this required him to lean over her so that he could smell the scent of her—baby powder and tea and chalk.

He inhaled, his nose coming within inches of her forehead. *This* was the reason why he didn't want women in the shop. Too distracting, and being distracted led to injuries.

When he managed to step away from her, he saw that she'd tucked her lower lip under her teeth with enough pressure that the flesh was bleaching white. What had been, up to that moment, a mere irritating attraction shifted right over to desire. He wanted the pretty little schoolteacher in a way that had nothing to do with civility. He wanted to kiss the color back into her lip, to find out how hard she was capable of biting.

Then she looked up at him through thick lashes, and he saw his own desire mirrored in her eyes. She wasn't scared of him, nor was she mad at him. As difficult as it was to believe, she wanted him, too.

Either that, or the goggles were distorting her eyes. Just like that, Billy felt the way he had when he'd been introduced to her at Ben and Josey's wedding—tongue-tied, unsure of what to do next.

Uncertainty was not a feeling he was comfortable with, especially not when it was stomping on some good old-fashioned temptation. So he forced himself to turn away from her and do the one thing he was always comfortable doing.

He got back to work.

Five

Jenny hadn't slept much. Her ears still burned where Billy had touched her with the barest hint of pressure. She couldn't get past how gentle his touch had been—or how much it had affected her. She'd have expected a man like him to be all rough, very tumble. But soft, tender caresses? Coupled with the heated looks he kept giving her?

No amount of tossing and turning in her bed had let her sleep.

"Billy said that he's going to let me help weld the frame," Seth repeated for the fourth time that morning.

Yawning, she turned the final corner, looking for Billy's bike. It wasn't in the parking lot, which left her feeling vaguely disappointed, but then Seth said, "That's his truck!"

Maybe it was. And it was parked right next to her spot.

She rolled up and came to a stop before she looked in the cab. Well, tried to, anyway. The truck sat a good two feet above her. Black, of course. She expected nothing less from Billy Bolton.

"Morning," Billy said as he rounded his truck and opened her door for her.

The gentlemanly act threw her for another loop, but if he was insulted that she sat there staring at him in the dawning morning, he didn't show it.

"Hey, where's your bike?" Seth got out of the car.

"Had to bring pipe," Billy said as he closed Jenny's door behind her, turned and opened up the passenger door of his truck. "Brought you some tea."

"Really?" She caught herself. "I mean, thank you."

"You're welcome," he replied, handing her a cup from a fancy coffeehouse she couldn't afford.

This time, Jenny's fingers had to linger over his, not the other way around. This time, she was the one who was doing the touching. This time, she let herself feel the span of his fingers. They were thick, but long. Perfectly balanced for their size.

Just like Billy.

She needed to say something—anything—to extricate herself from this situation. "How much do I owe you?"

It was hard to make out his features in the early-morning light, but she thought he raised an eyebrow at her—the same look he'd given her when she'd caught him stripping off his shirt in front of her class. "You don't owe me anything, Jenny."

"What do you need pipe for? I thought we cut the pipe for the frame last night? Aren't we going to weld it?"

She pulled her hand—and the tea—away from Billy and walked away from the narrow space between their vehicles.

On the one hand, Jenny was thankful for Seth's interruption. He was keeping her from doing something completely stupid, like continually touching Billy Bolton. Because that would be bad. Somehow.

On the other, she wanted to strangle her boy. Things with Billy had such interesting potential—potential that was always interrupted by a teenager or a bike. Yes, she was pitifully out of practice at flirting, but even an old pro would find it challenging in this situation.

"Whoa. We *might* get to welding after school today—if your mother says it's okay." As he opened the gate on the truck, Billy looked at her for approval.

"As long as he's got all the safety gear," Jenny replied, taking a sip of her tea. Lightly sweetened black tea. Still warm enough to be hot. Perfect, she thought with a satisfied sigh.

"But everyone else gets a crack at cutting pipe, too. Bobby says it'll look good for the camera. So the rest of the kids get to cut junk pipe. And you," he added, pointing a finger at Seth, "get to carry it all to the shop. Get started."

"Me? Why?"

"This is the grunt work, kid. And you are the grunt."

Jenny managed not to laugh at this keen observation. Mumbling under his breath about how this *totally* wasn't fair, Seth hauled out a few lengths of pipe and began carrying them to the shop. He dropped one, then another. Juggling the remaining pipe, he tried to kick the pipes on the ground, but only succeeded in stubbing his toe.

"Let him handle it," Billy said, close to her ear as his massive hand settled on her shoulder and pulled her back—gently—toward the truck.

Too late, she realized she'd gasped, although she would have been hard-pressed to say if her response was out of concern for Seth or because of the sudden pressure of Billy's touch.

She wanted to squirm—this was different than the last time he'd held her back. Instead of the middle of the well-lit shop, with a camera recording their every move, she was alone with Billy in the dark.

She tensed. Would he press her against the truck's side, all of those tattooed muscles giving her no place to go?

Would he take a kiss from her—or something more? Would she let him?

Good girls didn't let bad boys take those kisses, and Jenny had spent the past fourteen years being a good girl. Through hard work and dedication, she'd become a respectable woman—*not* someone who chased rich bad boys.

So why did she want him to kiss her so much?

Darn it all, he didn't do any of that. Instead, he trailed his hand down her back—which still made her insides quiver, especially when his hand traced the curve of her hips, just above her bottom.

God, she needed to say something. Anything.

"I…" Then she looked up, her gaze meeting Billy's.

His face was only a few inches from hers, and the look in his eyes melted the part of her brain that was trying to engage in polite conversation.

Billy grinned. Not a full-on display of teeth, just the corners of his mouth moving up in unison, but he looked as if he'd discovered the cookie jar and was about to stick his hand into it.

"This is the part," he said, his voice rumbling out of his broad chest as he reached up and smoothed her hair away from her face, "where you threaten to feed me to the coyotes."

Ah. Yes, that was her line. But she was powerless to say that, much less anything else. All she could think was, *dance with me. Dance with me and make it worth it.*

Then the sound of metal clanging on metal and what was most likely an inappropriate curse word muttered by her son snapped her out of her stupor. Seth was still about, after all. It wouldn't do to have him see his mother and this man making googly eyes at each other.

She pulled away. It took more effort than she thought it would.

"How you doing?" Billy called out, looking none the worse for wear.

"This is stupid," came the completely Seth-like response.

"You don't have to haul metal," Billy responded, still looking completely unflustered. "You also don't have to help with the welding. Your call, kid."

Seth stomped up to the truck, gave Billy the dirty look that was all-too-familiar to Jenny, and grabbed another couple of pipes.

"I carried metal when I was your age," Billy called out after him. "Builds character."

"Whatever."

This time, Jenny did giggle. She should have been irritated that Seth was snotty to Billy, but honestly, it was a relief to know that he wasn't like that only with her. And to know there were limits to Billy's ability to charm the boy.

Even if there didn't appear to be limits on how much he could charm her.

"What?" he asked over the lip of his cup.

"You're better at this than I thought you would be."

This hung out there for a moment. Truthfully, he was better at a lot of things than she would have given him credit for. Working with the kids. Managing Seth. Humoring Don.

Making her feel special. That was the biggest surprise of all.

After a heavy pause, he shrugged. "Shop is good for kids."

"Oh?"

He nodded. "You may have trouble believing this, but I wasn't exactly a perfect student back when I was his age."

"No!" she gasped in mock surprise, which made him chuckle. "Actually, neither was I." After all, she'd already lost her virginity by Seth's age. That's how a girl wound up pregnant at fifteen.

But then the silence between them stretched, and she realized that he was staring at her. And she remembered that he'd asked her how old she was, how old Seth was.

"That was a long time ago," she hurried to add, feeling the kind of shameful embarrassment she hadn't had time to feel in years. Then, after the words were out, she realized they made her sound old.

Maybe she should drink her tea.

"Interesting," he muttered as Seth stomped up, grabbed more pipes and hauled them off. When he was out of earshot, Billy continued—by tucking her hair behind her ears again.

There was no way in heck her hair was that messy this early in the morning. But she couldn't pull away. The pads of his fingertips grazed her earlobe and moved down her jawline with a steady pressure.

"What is?"

"You. I even look at your boy funny, and you'll rip my liver out and leave it for the vultures. But I look at you?" He leaned in—so close that she could feel the warmth of his breath on the side of her face as his fingers lifted her chin. "I look at you, I ask about you, I *touch* you—you curl up in your shell, like one of those crabs."

"I'm not a crab," she managed to get out.

"Says the woman who promised to feed me to the coyotes." She could hear the laughter in his voice, even if he wasn't laughing. A man had no right sounding that sexy. Not when he was only inches from her, not when his fingertips had complete control over her. None.

He was going to kiss her. He was going to kiss her and Seth was going to walk up and see him kissing her and she didn't know why but she couldn't let Seth see her like that. She couldn't. She was a good mom. She did not lose her head over men. Not anymore. So she said the first thing her mind threw up in defense. "Maybe I'm just scared of you."

The moment the words left her mouth, he pulled back. The sun was up high enough now that she could see the way he shut down—his eyes went blank, almost mean-looking, as he crossed his arms. His whole attitude became one of sullen rebellion.

Seth trudged back up. "Last three," he said. "Now what?"

Billy looked at her from behind his mask of attitude for a pained moment before his body uncoiled. He grabbed the pipe out of Seth's hands and took off for the shop at a good clip. "We get to work."

Jenny watched them go, too stunned to say anything.

What the heck had just happened?

Billy had been wrong. That's all there was to it.

He'd misread Jenny. The huge, wide eyes? The lip biting? The pretty blushes? Not desire. Fear. His own wishful thinking had him thinking she wanted him, when in reality? He scared the crap out of her.

He'd thought she'd been different. Hell, he thought *he'd* been different—that he wasn't making the same mistakes judging women that he always made. He'd thought he was getting it right this time.

He'd been wrong. Again.

It wasn't like this was the first time he'd misjudged a woman. Hell, he'd thought Ashley loved him back when he was young and stupid. He'd loved her, at the very least— loved her and been willing to marry her, even though he'd only been seventeen, even though it had felt like his life would end if he got married and had a baby before he was old enough to vote, much less drink. Then Ashley had gone and had that abortion, had thrown it in his face when he'd been crushed and furious about her doing it without telling him. "I got rid of *it* because I didn't want *you*" is what she'd said during their fight, right before she walked out of his life for good.

Yeah, he'd misjudged women before. Maybe he'd never *not* misjudged one. Which was why he was thirty-four and still damned alone. Just him and his bikes.

In this foul mood, Billy found himself cutting pointless pipe all damn day long. He got into an argument with Don about whether or not the kids could take their lengths of pipe home as a souvenir. He snarled at Seth when the kid tried to adjust the saw like Billy had shown him the night before. And when Billy's kid brother Bobby shoved a camera in his face to get him cussing at little kids on film, Billy punched him in the gut.

None of that made him feel any better. If anything, he felt worse. He wanted to hit a bar and drink until he didn't feel anything at all. He used to do that all the time, back when he was still young. Back when he was trying to forget Ashley and the baby that wasn't and never would be. Back when he would throw down at the drop of a hat.

Back when the cops knew him on a first-name basis.

Those days were long gone, though. He was too damn busy to spend his time drunk and brawling—he had the business to prove it. A business that provided him with a purpose—and more money than he knew what to do with and the "opportunity" to have his whole life filmed.

Yeah, he was in one hell of a bad mood.

The bell rang back in the main building and kids bailed. Billy sat in the shop, brooding. If Seth knew what was good for him, he'd steer clear today.

Kids never did seem to know what was good for them.

"Um, Billy? Mr. Bolton?" Seth poked his head around the door. "Are we going to weld today? On the frame?"

"No. Go home."

How had he gotten it so wrong? Of course he scared

her. She was a soft, delicate little woman—sensitive and pretty—and he was, well, he was still a badass biker, covered in ink. Nothing would ever be able to change that basic fact—not the money he'd made or how unwillingly famous he'd become.

"I can still sweep up…"

"Go. Home."

What the hell was wrong with him? He didn't go for women like Jenny Wawasuck—women who were smart and cared about kids. Who put other people first. The women he normally went for were women who weren't surprised that Wild Bill Bolton was, in fact, a little wild.

"Look, if this is about this morning, I'm sorry. It won't happen again."

Billy's attention snapped back on Seth as the kid edged into the room. "What?"

Seth looked as if he was on the verge of throwing up. "I wasn't trying to make you mad. I don't mind carrying pipes. I won't complain next time."

If this were just a misunderstanding between him and Jenny, well, that would suck enough. But the additional layer of the kid mucked everything up. Billy had half a mind to toss the boy out on his rear, but the moment the thought occurred to him, guilt hit him upside the head. Would Cal Horton, his shop teacher in high school, have thrown Billy out because Cal had had a bad day teaching? No. No matter what was going on with Cal, he was there when Billy needed an adult to talk to. If it hadn't been for Cal, Billy would be rotting in prison. If he weren't dead.

It wasn't this kid's fault that Billy couldn't read a woman. Even if that woman was the boy's mother. Damn. "I don't want to hear a lot of lip."

Seth's face brightened. "Understood."

Billy regarded him for a moment longer. Shop had saved him, back in school—shop and Cal. When Billy had finally made good and done something with his life, he'd promised Cal that he'd pay it forward.

"Suit up, kid. Let's weld."

Six

She was just checking on her son. That was all. Not talking to Billy Bolton, not touching Billy Bolton, not even *looking* at Billy Bolton.

The only person she was concerned with was Seth. That's how it had been for the past fourteen years. She didn't have time in her life to have her head spun around by a dangerous man. She didn't have time to wonder why she said the things she did, why she *did* the things she did. Her number one priority was shepherding Seth through adolescence and making sure he stayed on the straight and narrow. That's what good moms did.

Her walking out to the shop after her TAPS meeting had nothing to do with the way Billy's face changed when he grinned at her or how her body begged her to dance with him every time he traced a finger over her skin. Heavens, it certainly had nothing to do with the way he focused on everything about her with such a laserlike intensity that he could tell she only drank tea by catching her scent.

No, she was not thinking about that. She was thinking about Seth.

The shop door was locked.

She jiggled the doorknob again, but it wasn't her imagi-
nation—the thing was locked tight. Then she noticed the
sign on the door—Welding. Do Not Enter—written in a
heavy scrawl and fixed to the door with duct tape.

"Seth? Billy? Open up!"

The door swung open. Seth stood there, a welding helmet on his head, the visor part swung up. "What?"

She was a little taken aback by his appearance. Wearing
a heavy jacket and an apron so long it covered his feet, he
looked like he was dressed for battle, not shop. He looked…
almost grown up. "What are you two doing in here?"

He gave her that special teenager look—the one that said
she was a complete idiot. "Welding, Mom. Duh. Didn't you
see the sign?" But then he cracked a smile. "It's *so* cool!"

Okay, so even if she'd made Billy mad this morning—
and she still wasn't sure what, exactly, had been the straw
that broke that camel's back—it was a relief to know that
Billy was still honoring his promise to Seth.

."I want to talk to Billy."

"We're busy." Seth started to close the door on her, but
she jammed her foot into the gap and gave him her no-
monkey-business look.

"Let me in, Seth."

"Can't. Don't have enough gear for you, and Billy says
everyone has to have gear if they're going to be around
welding."

"Where's Don?"

"Left after school. Mom, we're busy." He started to shut
the door on her foot.

"You tell Mr. Bolton I want to talk to him. *Now.*"

Seth hesitated for a moment before he buckled. "Fine,
but you gotta wait here. You don't have any gear." At least
he left the door open a crack.

Jenny peeked into the shop. Billy was dressed much
like Seth was, except Billy's gear fit him better. The mo-

ment he turned his shielded head in her direction, he fired up the blowtorch.

Even though she couldn't see his eyes behind the darkened glass of his mask, she could feel him staring at her. If he was trying to intimidate her, he was succeeding. When he wanted to, the man could be positively menacing. Nothing she saw before her was even vaguely reminiscent of the thoughtful man who'd brought her tea and whispered in her ear this morning. She swallowed down her nerves. Clearly, she'd angered him. Even more clearly, she wanted to avoid doing that again in the future.

She still wasn't sure what had set him off. All she'd said was that maybe she was afraid of him. Why would that have upset him so much? It'd only been one little conditional clause, for Pete's sake—*maybe*. Because she wasn't actually afraid of him—she'd just been desperate to keep from kissing him in front of Seth.

Seth clomped over to Billy—from the back, she could see he was wearing huge work boots—and spoke to him. The flame clicked off long enough for Billy to respond— or at least, that's what it looked like. Then the blowtorch was blowing again. Definitely not a man she had to worry about kissing at this exact moment.

Seth came back over, looking irritated with her. "He's busy."

Okay, so he was unhappy with her. But he was still interacting with her son, and she had a right to check in on them. "You tell him I want to talk to him when he's done being 'busy.' I'll be in my classroom." Then, rather than wait around for another menacing flash from the blowtorch, she turned and headed back to her room.

The *maybe* bothered her. He'd heard the *maybe,* right? He had to have known that she wasn't being serious, right?

Maybe. Maybe not.

They weren't done here. Not by a long shot.

* * *

For the first time in a long time, Billy pulled open the doors to a school and stepped inside.

He couldn't believe he was doing this—walking into her classroom, on *her* turf.

It was easy to figure out which room was hers. Only one door was open, only one light was on. Everyone else had left hours ago. She got here first, stayed last. All she did was teach.

Just like all he did was build bikes for insane amounts of money.

He knew that she heard him coming. He'd never been exactly light on his feet. The sound of his steel-toe boots echoed down the otherwise silent halls. There was no turning back. He was all in for this little dressing down or whatever she had in mind—he knew it wouldn't be pretty.

Taking a deep breath, he turned into her classroom. The first—the only—things he saw were her legs. She was standing on a chair, trying to tack up some sort of border over the blackboard. As she reached over her head and stood on her tiptoes, the length of her calves, below the hem of her skirt, weren't exactly at eye level, but they were on more prominent display than normal. His blood ran hot. Nice legs. *Great* legs, he thought before he caught himself. That was exactly the kind of thinking that had gotten him in trouble this morning.

"Oh, good, you're here," she said, without turning around. "Can you hold this up for me?" She gestured toward a sagging section of paper. "Please," she added, almost as an afterthought.

He stood there for a moment—not because he was uncertain of what was going on. That wasn't it. More like he was admiring her backside, all tight and cupped by her skirt.

"Won't take long, Billy," she said, and he didn't hear

"scared" in her voice. He heard gentle teasing. And maybe something else—the same thing he'd deluded himself into thinking he'd heard for the past few days. Attraction. Desire.

He felt ridiculous standing this close to her, paper border in hand. She arranged the border to her liking and stapled it up. Then she handed him the stapler. "If you don't mind, since you're down there." And she smiled at him. Because of the chair, she was practically looking him straight in the eyes.

He didn't have the first clue about what to do. If he were his brother Ben, he'd come up with something logical to say that would get him out of this. If he were his brother Bobby, he'd make a move on her.

But he wasn't either. So he did some stapling and forced himself to look anywhere but at her.

Billy was trying so hard not to look at her that when she put her hands on his shoulders, he jumped. With a little bit of force, she turned him to face her. "You don't, you know."

He swallowed. "I don't what?"

"You don't scare me." She ran her tongue over her lower lip. It made her look hungry.

"Sure I do. You said so yourself."

Her hands slid from his shoulders toward his neck with a slow, sure pressure. "Maybe. There was a *maybe* in that sentence. Which means there's a *maybe not*."

She was pulling him in closer, and he'd be damned if he was powerless to stop her. She looked like she was going to kiss him and it looked like he was going to let her.

"Then why did you say it?" Shoot, his voice wasn't tough or even scary. It was something low and deep, but quiet, a voice that he rarely heard himself use—unless he was trying to sweet-talk a woman. And if he was trying to sweet-talk this woman, even he had to admit he was doing a poor job of it.

"Because I didn't want to do *this* in front of Seth."

She pulled him into her and kissed him. Her lips crushed against his with enough force that he let out a low groan. Man, she smelled so good, felt even better.

She kissed with her eyes closed. Billy knew this because he was so stunned that he couldn't do anything but stare at her. Her cheeks were flushed a delicate pink, which made her look soft. Beautiful. Innocent.

Innocent women didn't kiss him.

Which meant this had to be either a mistake or the most dangerous game of chicken he'd ever played.

Was she trying to prove that she wasn't afraid of him? Fine. He'd had that happen to him before, back when he was wild and crazy. For a long time, he'd enjoyed the attention. It'd felt good to have women throw themselves at him, even if it led to a lot of bar brawls with angry boyfriends. Every time he started making out with some nameless woman on a Saturday night, he'd felt like shoving Ashley's face in it—see? Other women wanted him. Other women *fought* over him.

It had been an ego trip—for a while. Then the nameless, faceless kissing—often followed by some nameless, faceless sex? It left him hurting more than any hangover ever would. So he'd stopped doing it. Going to bars, picking up women, getting drunk every other night—all of it.

Maybe that was why he hadn't done any dating after making the business a success. True, the business *was* a success because he stayed out of the bars. But when high-society women hit on him at the functions Bobby or Ben made him attend, it reminded him of how hollow he'd felt back in the day.

Which meant he was out of practice. If he were in a bar now, more than a little drunk, he'd pick Jenny up and push her against a wall. Because what he wanted was to sink into the softness of her body and forget everything but the woman who had a hold of him.

But he wasn't in a bar. He was standing in a classroom. And he would not rise to her bait. Although his body wasn't exactly paying attention to that direct order.

At the very least, he wasn't going to sweep her off that chair and pull her into his chest. He wasn't going to do anything like that, because if he did, he knew damn good and well that he *would* scare the hell out of her. She had no idea what kind of fire she was playing with.

Then she traced his lips with the tip of her tongue, and Billy's resolve weakened. Hell, everything weakened. He was physically shaking from holding his arms at his sides, when all he wanted to do was wrap them around her.

She was beautiful kissing him—so beautiful he wanted to step out of himself and watch the whole thing. He might never get another chance at this kind of sweetness.

Finally, she pulled back. Her lips parted, she was breathing heavily with her eyes still closed. Then she licked her lips again. She was trying to taste him, he realized. That made him want to kiss her again. He'd never wanted to kiss a woman so much.

Then her eyelids fluttered open, and he saw that look in her eyes—want. Pure and simple. She wanted him.

This would be the perfect time to fish a compliment out of the depths of his brain.

He had nothing. Instead, he said, "No kissing in front of the kid. Good rule."

A smile tugged at her mouth. She looked as if she was going to say something else, but then a door slammed.

"Hey, Billy," Seth called out, his voice echoing down the hall. Jenny's eyes shot wide with alarm. "I got the shop all swept."

Right. This would be test number one of the new no-kissing rule. Moving as fast as he could without pulling

Jenny off the chair, Billy stepped back and put a desk between them. Seconds later, Seth came bounding—there was no other word for it—into the room. "Oh, hey." He eyed them suspiciously.

"That border looks straight." It was the first thing that popped into Billy's mouth.

Jenny blinked at him before turning around. "Oh, yes. Great. Thanks for your help."

"Are we gonna weld again in the morning? I've got some boots at home. I'll wear those." At least the awkward moment didn't faze the kid.

"You do that."

Jenny climbed down off her chair. She wasn't exactly staring at the floor, but she wasn't exactly looking at him, either. But she wasn't afraid of him. That much he felt sure about now. She hadn't kissed him to prove a point. She'd kissed him because she wanted to.

That simple fact was more than enough to muddle his thinking. So when she ushered him and Seth outside and locked up the school, he found himself staring at her.

She caught him and rewarded him with one of her sunny smiles. "We'll see you tomorrow, right?"

"Yeah."

He watched them get in the car. He'd see them tomorrow.

Man, he couldn't wait to come back to school.

Seven

Billy got to the school extra early the next morning. He'd worked in his garage all night, as if he could *build* an eloquent response to Jenny. He wondered if he'd get another chance to kiss her today. Wasn't going to be easy. No kissing in front of her kid—or any other kid, for that matter—and no way in hell he was making a move on her anywhere near a camera. Which limited their options.

The bad news was that Jenny wasn't at school when he rolled up. The worse news? Bobby's sports car was. Damn. Billy was rarely in the mood to talk with his baby brother. He loved the guy, he did, but ever since Bobby had put Billy on camera he'd had trouble thinking charitable thoughts about the guy. Today was no exception.

Bobby was sitting at the worktable, sipping what was probably a twelve-dollar cup of coffee. At least he looked tired.

Bobby was everything Billy wasn't—handsome, smooth, smart, good with women—hell, good with people. And he always got his way. He had Bruce Bolton, their father, in his back pocket. Seriously, how many other people could just decide to put the family on a reality internet show and make it happen? Only Bobby. Everything he touched turned to gold.

This particular morning, Billy couldn't remember ever being as jealous of his little brother as he was right now. Bobby would know how to handle the situation with Jenny. But Billy wasn't about to ask his little brother for advice. That was the road straight to hell. So he stuck to the obvious. "What are you doing here?"

"I need a reason to hang out with you?"

"Before seven in the morning? Yeah, you do." To distract himself, Billy picked up the frame he and Seth had welded last night and tested the joints. They held. The kid's work wasn't half-bad.

"I wanted to talk to you." The only thing more dangerous than Bobby as a smooth talker was Bobby as a serious businessman. And that was his serious-business voice.

"Now what? Going to put cameras in my bedroom? Film me in the shower?"

When Bobby didn't have a snappy comeback, Billy knew he was screwed. He turned to his brother, frame still in hand. A man could do a lot of damage with some welded pipe. A *lot* of damage.

Bobby sat there, sipping his coffee as if this were another regular early-morning call. Maybe he hadn't done a good enough job keeping Jenny off the camera. No doubt Bobby wanted to develop the feelings Billy was having for the schoolmarm into some sort of plotline for his show.

"No way in hell—over my dead body."

"You don't even know what I'm going to ask you." Bobby had the nerve to smile. Billy wanted to cave his teeth in.

"Okay, fine. Ask away. The answer is *no*."

"The footage looks good. You're doing well with that boy—what's his name?"

"Seth." Billy didn't so much say it as growl it.

"Yes, yes. Seth. I think women are going to go wild for this new, softer side of you."

Billy snorted. He didn't want "women" to go wild for him. Just the one.

That thought took him by such surprise that he didn't have a snappy comeback for what Bobby said next. "I've been in talks with the owner of the FreeFall network—heard of them?"

"I don't watch TV."

"You might have to start." Bobby grinned like some sort of fool, which made Billy think that was supposed to have been a joke. He wasn't laughing. "The man's name is David Caine. He's interested in picking up the show as a midseason replacement. If we can make the magic number of hits for the webisodes."

Billy wished he had gotten some sleep, because as it was, he couldn't be sure that this wasn't a nightmare. "You're serious? Filming me and putting it on the web isn't enough?"

"This is huge, Billy."

"I don't want to be famous." Fame was making it extra hard to figure out how to court a nice, normal woman like Jenny. Fame was making him twitchy. Fame was ruining his life. "You're the one who wants to be famous. Why don't you film yourself?"

"I'm not as interesting as you are." Billy rolled his eyes at this, but Bobby continued. "You make these awesome bikes and you don't take crap from anyone." Was that a compliment? A sincere one? But then Bobby ruined it by adding, "Not even first-grade teachers with attitude problems."

"You watch your mouth." It came out so fast that Billy didn't have time to realize what he was saying.

Bobby's eyes widened. "You *like* her?"

He could see the wheels in Bobby's head turning. Bobby

would try to strong-arm Jenny into playing out their little flirtation—or whatever the hell it was—on camera.

"Well. That's…interesting." Boy, Billy hated that grin. "But that's not what I want to talk to you about."

"It isn't?" That wasn't like the twit, to have an advantage and not press it. The warning bells in Billy's head got a little louder.

"Josey said I have to get your approval for this."

"Approval for what?"

"You're building that bike to be auctioned off for the school, correct?" He gestured to the frame Billy had forgotten he was still holding.

"Yeah…" Any second now, it'd hit—the catch. There was always a catch.

"I've come up with a way to auction the bike that's going to maximize both our profit and our exposure level."

"What the hell does that mean?"

Bobby smiled again, but this time Billy could tell he was nervous. "It means that, when we auction off the chopper, I think we should also auction off some bachelors."

Before Billy could process that, Bobby stood and began pacing. "Hear me out. You're the reason we're getting the views we've been getting, but we need to hit it hard. What better way to sell you to the highest bidder for a night? We'd have a packed house of who's who. Hell, we could invite some of our celebrity customers. You know how high-society people like to buy things for charity. Plus, we'd get our webisode hits—gruff biker in a tux!—and we'd raise a hell of a lot of money for the school." He paused and turned to face Billy, beaming like an idiot. "Everyone wins!"

After several moments, Billy became aware that he was standing with his jaw hanging about midchest. Out of all the ludicrous things he'd ever heard—including making him an internet star—this took the cake. "Are you on drugs?"

Bobby's smile cracked a little. "It won't be just you. Dad said we could auction him off, and me, of course." He puffed out his chest a little. "Ben's out, though. Josey was firm about that. But the guys in Ben's band already said yes. I have a few other leads on eligible, *willing* bachelors. All I need is you."

"*Josey* thinks this is a good idea?" Their sister-in-law was an all-around down-to-earth woman. But she was also a corporate fund-raiser…. He was possibly screwed in the worst sort of way.

"Absolutely. I did a little research, put together a spreadsheet for her showing the kind of returns these sorts of events bring in. She was impressed."

"Let me see it." Not that he loved spreadsheets, but it must have been a hell of a file to sway Josey.

Bobby looked dumbfounded. "I didn't bring it."

Billy wanted to pummel his brother. Ben—the *good* brother—went over the company financial statements with Billy every month and they discussed Billy's portfolio every three months. He knew exactly where the company stood and which investments his own money was tied up in. He may not know what to do with it all, but he knew where it was. "There's no way in hell you can auction me off to the highest bidder."

Bobby's smile turned scheming. "A bachelor auction has the potential to raise another fifty thousand bucks for the school, *William*. You know who'd like another fifty grand? A certain teacher would probably *love* some additional money to buy supplies. I imagine those kids go through a lot of crayons. You want me to tell her you said no to more school supplies for those tykes?"

So that's what this was—blackmail. "I'll buy her a box of crayons. I'm not going to be auctioned off."

Bobby was ready for him. "You know who else would love a bigger budget? Don. He was telling me how he wants an after-school program for the boys—part sports, part shop, part keeping them out of trouble. He doesn't have any money for it now. You could change that."

Billy glared at his little brother. Of course he'd use Billy's love of shop against him. If Billy had had a program like that, he probably wouldn't have gotten his high school girlfriend pregnant, and probably wouldn't have been such a screwup that she'd known what a terrible father he would have made. If only Billy had had something like that, his whole life might have turned out differently.

He had plenty of money. Maybe he could ask Ben to move some of it around. Hell, he'd rather just cut the school a check than be a part of a bachelor auction. Bobby was looking at him, expecting Billy to agree to being bought and sold for what was little more than a ratings stunt.

"Go to hell, creep."

"Come *on,* man! I'm talking about one night of your life. I hadn't realized how selfish you are."

Billy was selfish? After he agreed to make his life a matter of public record for the sake of the family business? After he agreed to foot the bill for a custom-built chopper to auction off for the school? Hell, *no.*

Billy had never played football. He'd been plenty tough, but he'd never had grades that were even close enough for the coaches to look the other way. Both his brothers had, though. Which is why Bobby should have seen the hit coming.

Billy dropped the frame and covered the distance—maybe ten feet—between him and Bobby before the metal clanged on the ground. With a satisfying "Oomf!" Billy hit his baby brother with enough force that they moved the worktable a good six feet before forward momentum stopped.

They'd always done this—fighting, Mom had called it. Dad insisted it was harmless tussling and never broke it up. Some days, Bobby came out on top—he was a fast sucker and had a solid left hook. But he couldn't match Billy for sheer strength.

"I'll build bikes for you and your little show, but that doesn't give you the right to sell me on the open market. You got that?"

Behind them, a door slammed and someone gasped. Crap. Billy had forgotten about Seth. He dropped Bobby and spun around to see Seth's eyeballs all but jumping out of his head. "Hey."

"You, uh, you guys okay? I can come back later...." Seth edged for the door.

Billy shot Bobby a warning glance. Had Bobby connected the kid to Jenny? He hoped not. Manslaughter was a serious crime.

"No, we're done here. Right, Bobby?"

Bobby cleared his throat, gave Billy's shoulder a half-hearted slug and straightened out what was left of his shirt. "We're all good. Just messing around, kiddo. Brothers are like that."

Seth gave Bobby a look. "Yeah, whatever, mister." Then he turned his attention back to Billy. "Are we still going to weld?" He held up his booted foot to display his preparation.

"I'll leave you two to it." Bobby headed for the door at a respectable clip.

"Hey!" Billy yelled after him. He'd long since learned that if he didn't get a hard promise out of Bobby, the guy took it as a victory.

Bobby stopped, hand on the door. Then he turned back. "Fine. You won't do it."

Billy doubted that was the final word, though.

Eight

"What are we going to do tonight?" Jenny asked the fourteen girls sitting in her classroom. They were between eight and eighteen. Nine of them were pregnant.

"No drinking, no drugs," they chanted in unison. All except Cyndy in the back.

"And?" she prompted, keeping an eye on Cyndy.

"Do our homework, go to school tomorrow."

"Good job, girls. Remember—call me if you need to. Otherwise, I'll see you tomorrow, right?" Everyone gathered their things, snagged the last of the cookies to go and headed out. Except Cyndy.

She hadn't said anything during the TAPS meeting, which was unusual. Her eyes and nose were red. Jenny hoped that she hadn't skipped school today and gotten high. She sat beside the girl, waiting. Cyndy was still here, so there was still hope.

"I can't do this, Jenny." Cyndy threw herself into Jenny's arms, the sobs ripping through her. "I just can't."

Jenny's throat caught. Cyndy was only a year older than Jenny had been when she'd gotten pregnant. "What happened, honey?"

"Tige broke up with me. He doesn't care about me or the baby."

Yeah, she'd been there, too. Some days were good days—a girl had a healthy baby, another girl didn't get pregnant.

But today? Today was not one of the good days. Today was going to break her heart.

"Oh, honey." Of course, she hadn't figured Tige would man up. But telling Cyndy that would be pouring salt in the wound, and that wasn't her job here. Her job was to keep Cyndy from doing something that she'd spend the rest of her life regretting.

"My mom says I have to give it up and my grandma says that if I give it up then it won't be a Lakota anymore," Cyndy wept. "But I don't want to have it. I can't."

Jenny was going to have a talk with Bertha Speaks Fast. "No matter where that baby is," she said, patting Cyndy's seven-month-pregnant stomach, "it'll always be Lakota."

"I can't" was all Cyndy could say.

"Did you get high today? Drink?" When the girl shook her head no, Jenny exhaled in relief. "I'm sorry, honey, it's too late for an abortion."

As a rule, Jenny didn't support abortion. But she'd seen too many babies born with Fetal Alcohol Syndrome or addicted to drugs, too many babies who were neglected and abused because their parents didn't know that they had to feed or change a crying infant. Reality dictated that she keep all options open.

Jenny's mother had made her keep her baby and had made darned sure Jenny didn't mess up everyone's life. Everything she'd learned about being a mother had come from Frances Wawasuck.

When Cyndy's sobs had finally subsided into hiccups, Jenny said, "Honey, you have to do what's right for you and for your baby. If you want to keep it, your family and the tribe will be here for you. If you decide to place the baby with a loving family, then I'll put you in touch with an adoption counselor. There's no right or wrong here."

This brought on more tears. Jenny rubbed her back. "Go home and get some sleep. Tomorrow, *after* you go to school, we'll make a plan."

"Okay," the girl sniffled.

"One day at a time." Jenny wrapped up the last cookie and sent Cyndy home.

Then she turned her attention to the envelope from the South Dakota Department of Social Services. *Please be a check,* she prayed as she opened it. When she'd started TAPS, she'd had enough funding to serve a hot meal to the girls every afternoon. It was the only dinner some of them got. She got a small stipend out of it, too, most of which had gone directly into Seth's college fund. The rest had gone to a new-car fund.

However, the state was behind on its bills. Months behind. She'd cut the meals back, but it hadn't taken long before she couldn't pay the cook to stay late. Now she was paying for milk and cookies out of her own pocket. Soon, she wouldn't even be able to do that.

She refused to give up hope. These girls—girls in a difficult spot like she'd been—needed an adult they could trust. Some of them had involved parents or grandparents, but most of them didn't. If Jenny hadn't had her mom, God only knew where she'd be now. Certainly not a college graduate with a good job, able to take care of herself and her son.

That's what she wanted all the girls to have, too. A chance to become the women they wanted to be. To that end, Jenny gave them unconditional support, a strict set of well-being rules and made darned sure they got the most education they could. After the babies came, the girls could keep coming to the meetings. This was a safe place for them, and Jenny was going to keep it that way, come hell or high water.

So she took a deep breath and opened the envelope. Her heart sank as she read the brief letter. Not only would the state be unable to pay its months-old debt, it wasn't even going to try. And there would be no more money.

Her program—her mission—was officially dead.

She couldn't stop, though. That would mean leaving girls like Cyndy twisting in the wind.

She gathered her things and turned off the light in her room. If she stopped buying cookies, she could stretch the money left in Seth's college fund to cover milk for several more months—at least through the New Year. Long enough to make sure Cyndy and a few of the other girls safely delivered their babies. And after that?

Lost in thought, Jenny straightened the room and peeked out the window. The production truck was gone, but the door to the shop was open and light spilled out. At least Billy was still here. Kissing him yesterday had been... well, it had been *something*. It had been years since she'd kissed a man. No, wait—scratch that. She'd never kissed a man. Only boys who thought they were men. Boys slept with girls and abandoned them. Men took responsibility for their actions.

Billy, she sensed, was a man.

She honestly couldn't tell if he'd liked the kiss or not and before she could figure it out, Seth had come in.

But...she'd put herself out there. *Way* out there. She'd liked the feel of Billy's lips against hers—heck, she hadn't even minded the way his beard scratched at her chin. There'd been something deliciously naughty about it— which had to be why it felt so out of character. Jenny Wawasuck didn't mess around. And yet...

True, a kiss was just that, but she'd managed to fluster

herself so badly that she hadn't even been able to bring herself to deliver a cup of tea out to Billy this morning.

But that's where she was headed now—the shop. Today she wasn't even trying to lie to herself that this was about Seth.

She'd had a long day. She wanted to see Billy, to have him give her one of those looks, those light touches, that set her heart racing. She wanted to forget about budget cuts and unborn babies and that constant feeling of treading water but never quite getting anywhere.

Seth was sweeping up already. Talking with Cyndy must have taken longer than she'd realized. Billy sat at his table, studying what she assumed were plans. In the middle of the floor sat a hunk of welded metal that, at the moment, looked nothing like a motorcycle.

"Hey," Seth said, sweeping his pile of dirt out of her way as she headed for the table. "I just started."

"No rush, sweetie."

"Mom..."

Right, right. Guys who built things probably didn't get called "sweetie" in the shop. Billy looked up at her and smiled. Sort of. It was one of those looks where the corners of his mouth crooked up almost imperceptibly. But she perceived it anyway.

She gestured toward the angular metal on the ground. "Looks good."

His lips moved even more. Oh, yes, he was smiling. Some of the tension of her day melted away. "You can tell that, huh?"

"Oh, sure. Very...metallic."

His gaze drifted down to her lips and back up, which sent a shot of heat through her.

Maybe yesterday, she'd taken him by surprise. Maybe today, *he'd* kiss *her*.

Except for Seth. So she redirected. "How was your day? I saw your brother was here early."

The warmth drained from Billy's face. "It was a day. You?"

When was the last time someone had asked her about her day—someone who wasn't her mother? "Long," she admitted with a shrug.

"Anything I can do to help?"

The way he said it—all serious, with an intent look on his face that made it clear that he would quite possibly do whatever she asked—left her feeling a little unsteady. In the best way possible.

"Not unless you've got a few extra thousand dollars lying around," she joked. "The funding for my after-school program got cut, and they aren't going to pay the overdue bills." But he didn't take it as a joke. Instead, his scowl deepened—like it had yesterday, when she'd carelessly lobbed out her "Maybe."

"What?"

"It always comes down to money, doesn't it?" He slammed his hand on the table, making all of the tools and things rattle about. "That's all anyone ever wants. Money."

He glared at her, but she refused to back down. "I'm not asking you to pay for TAPS, you know. I thought we were having a conversation."

"I'm already building this bike. I'm already giving my time to the school. I don't have anything else to give." It was more of a snarl than a statement, punctuated by another smack on the table.

"You're trying to scare me again, but it won't work," she said in a low voice so that Seth wouldn't hear her. She leaned in closer to Billy. "I'm not afraid of you."

Then the strangest thing happened. Billy Bolton, currently the meanest-looking man she knew, blushed. And not one of those delicate reddening of the cheeks—oh, no. He shot hot pink, the color turning his ears an unusual shade of red. Heck, even his neck—the part she could see—turned red.

The next thing she knew, he was up and moving, heading for the door with his head down, like a bull ready to do some damage to a neighborhood china shop.

She followed him out into the dim evening light. He'd covered a good deal of ground before he came to a stop, head down and hands on his hips. Not that he had hips. But, from this angle, she could see that he had a heck of a backside. One that, no doubt, matched all the muscles she'd seen a few days ago.

He heard her coming. "You should be, you know," he said without raising his head. "You should be very afraid of me."

"Give me one good reason." She circled around him.

"I'm not a nice guy, Jenny. I'm not even a good one. I have the reputation and the arrest record to prove it. No amount of money will ever change that. If you knew what was good for you and that boy of yours, you'd run from me right now."

He said it not as if he were proud of it, but as though he was resigned to carrying that burden of toughness for the rest of his life. He sounded tired.

Arrest record? She swallowed. Surely Josey would have mentioned something about a rap sheet before she agreed to let Billy work with children? Jenny knew a smart woman would probably take his advice and bail. He'd given voice to her worst fears—or at least, the fears she'd had a few days ago. Funny how much could change in a week.

She stepped in closer and saw the tension ripple through his shoulders. Moving slowly, she put her hand on his chest. She'd pushed him—or tried to, anyway—in that same spot on the first day. That had been the first time he'd confused her, when instead of pushing her back, he'd held on to her.

Like he did now. His fingers covered hers, and he pressed her hand into his chest. It was not the touch of a violent, dangerous man, no matter what he tried to tell her.

With her other hand, she ran her fingertips down his cheek, over his beard, and under his chin before she pulled his face up. "I am *not* afraid of you," she repeated in a breathy whisper.

This time, his hands cradled her waist. This time, he was going to dance with her. "You should be," he replied, pulling her in closer. "You *should* be."

"I'm not."

Later, she would be hard-pressed to say if she kissed him or if he kissed her. Later, all she would be able to say for certain was that she'd been hard-pressed against all of those muscles. Against Billy.

If yesterday's kiss had been nice, this one was a revelation. Her knees buckled under the force of Billy's mouth, but it didn't matter. He not only held her, but he also lifted her up as if she weighed next to nothing. She could feel his desire coiled below the surface of his skin as if he were waiting to unleash it all on her.

There were no confusing looks or miscommunicated ideas. This was a statement. He wanted her—all of her. It didn't matter that she had a teenaged son or was a boring schoolteacher or that she was perpetually broke. He still wanted her. In his arms, she felt lighter than a feather, lighter than air, even.

Despite the fact that he could pretty much do whatever he wanted with her, including throwing her over his shoulder and hauling her off—his tongue traced her lips, asking for permission. When she opened herself for him, though, he kissed her so hard that he almost bent her over backward.

As much as she didn't want that moment to end, she felt as though she were losing her balance. She pushed back.

He let her, but he didn't let go. Instead, he hugged her even harder. A deep rumble came directly out of his chest—the sound of pure satisfaction.

Folded within his muscular arms, she could feel his heart pounding through the fancy black T-shirt he wore. He was warm and solid and so strong it didn't matter that her feet weren't, in fact, on the ground. It felt like some part of her that she'd long ago shoved aside was waking up in his arms—the sensual, feminine part. She hugged him back, her face buried in the crook of his neck. The tang of metal and leather filled her nose, plus a deep, earthy musk that was his and his alone.

It ended slowly. First, he set her down, then he let her go. Each movement took several seconds, almost as if he was afraid that he'd never get this contact again.

As far as she was concerned, that wasn't an option. She smiled at him, feeling almost silly. "Feels a little naughty, kissing this close to the school."

He brushed her hair away from her face and cupped her cheek in his hand. "Maybe we should try to do that someplace else."

"Are you asking me out on a date?" The concept seemed foreign. Even when she'd been young and far too into boys, a formal request for a date had never happened. Other things had happened—obviously—but no one had ever asked her out before.

There it was again—that tired look. He was such a mystery to her. "I'm always working," he muttered, looking guilty.

"And I'm always at school."

"Not always. What do you do after you leave here?"

That struck a more hopeful note in her. "I cook dinner, do the dishes, hound Seth about his homework, talk to any girls that call and…fall into bed. And I do it all again the next day." He notched an eyebrow at her. It was a good look on him. "I catch up on house stuff on the weekends. Some of that stuff could keep, though…."

He nodded in understanding, then leaned down and kissed her forehead. It wasn't a huge thing, but the tenderness of it had her blushing again. "I'm going to ask you out on a date, Jenny, I promise. I want to take you out—someplace special. A night like you deserve."

God, that sounded wonderful—a night of nothing but her and him. A night like she hadn't had in, well, ever. "When?"

His chest heaved with a massive sigh. "The thing is, I've got to deal with my brother Bobby first. I don't want you on camera. You and I don't exist when there's a camera around."

At first, she was hurt by his words. How could they not exist after a searing kiss like that? But then the rest of what he'd said sunk in. They didn't exist *on camera.* He was protecting her.

"You can try to tell me you're not a good guy, but I know the real you, William Bolton." She turned her head and kissed the palm of his hand. "Let me know when you get it figured out. I'll be here."

She got a full-on smile that time. He practically beamed at her. One kiss—okay, it had been two kisses—wasn't going to be enough. She'd like to say that she hadn't felt this way in years, but honestly? She wasn't sure she'd ever felt this kind of pull for a man before. The way he made her body quiver with a gentle touch—to say nothing of the less-than-gentle touches—was something she was going to need a lot more of. The sooner the better. And, by the look on his face, he felt the same way.

"Yeah," he said, tracing her lips with his thumb, "I know where to find you."

Nine

As hard as it was, Jenny managed to wait until after Seth had closed his bedroom door before she bit the bullet and called Josey. Jenny didn't have a cell phone with all those unlimited anytime everybody minutes, so she saved calling Josey on her landline for emergencies.

And kissing Billy Bolton *after* he'd mentioned an arrest record was an emergency if she'd ever heard of one.

Josey answered on the third ring. "Hello?"

"It's me."

"You want me to call you back?"

Jenny smiled. Thanks to a trust fund, Josey had never hurt for money—and now that she was married to Ben Bolton, she never would. Still, she understood how the little things added up. Josey had unlimited anytime everybody minutes. It was thoughtful of her not to make Jenny pay for the call. "Yeah."

They hung up and Jenny sat, waiting. When her phone rang, she answered it before the end of the first ring.

"What's up? Is everything okay?"

Now *there* was a question Jenny would love to have an answer to. She opened her mouth to ask about Billy, but at the last second, she blinked. "It's official. Not only am I not getting any more TAPS funding from the state, but they're not going to bother covering back payments."

"Oh, no." Josey paused. "How much longer can you keep it going?"

Jenny rubbed her eyes. This was not the conversation she wanted to have. She wanted to know more about Billy, to find out that her trust in him wasn't totally misplaced. She wanted to not think about her mission in life dying a small, whimpering death at the hands of budget cuts.

"I don't know. I'd put most of the stipend in savings for Seth to go to college. If I start digging into that…I could maybe make it through part of the summer." Summer was the most important time to be there for the TAPS girls. Summer—with no school, no schedule—was when most of the girls got pregnant. It's when she'd gotten pregnant.

There was a long pause. Jenny couldn't guess what Josey was thinking. She'd never asked Josey for money before. Yes, Josey's very wealthy and very white grandfather had left her a trust fund—but she'd used almost all of it to pay for the school's construction. True, she was married to a very rich man, but Ben had also basically paid for the shop and all the equipment in it. She wasn't comfortable asking them for more.

At least, she was not comfortable asking them to cut her a check. But she was open to other ideas. If anything, the numbers man of the Bolton family should have some good ideas on how to fill the money gaps. Ben and Josey were a financial power couple. Josey was a professional corporate fund-raiser and Ben was a Chief Financial Officer. If anyone could get her out of this mess, it would be the two of them.

True to form, Josey said, "We can make sure you get something when we auction off the bike Billy's building."

"Yeah…about him."

"What about him? Is everything okay?"

"It's fine. Sort of."

"Jenny…"

Josey was as close to a sister as Jenny would ever have, which meant that there were very few things Jenny could hide from her. "Why didn't you tell me that Billy had an arrest record?"

"Oh, *that*."

"Yes, that."

"I didn't tell you because it wasn't important." When Jenny scoffed at this, Josey went on, "I mean it. He was arrested three times for public drunkenness, brawling and assault, which goes with public drunkenness and brawling, I think. But the last time was about ten years ago. He got probation and community service. Once he started seriously building bikes, he cleaned up and turned his life around." Josey dropped her voice to a whisper. "I know you're worried about him—he can *seem* really dangerous, but…"

"I'm not worried. He doesn't scare me." That defense was out before she could think better of it, and the thundering silence that followed was way, way louder than anything else Josey could have said.

Dang it. She'd overplayed her hand.

"How did you find out about his arrests?" Josey's voice was carefully casual—too casual. She probably could have pulled that tone on a stranger, but Jenny knew better. Josey was suddenly very interested in what Jenny thought of Billy.

She wouldn't be able to come up with a cover story on the fly that would convince her cousin. "He told me."

"Really." It wasn't a question. Jenny knew what Josey was going to say next before she even said it. "He doesn't usually tell people about that. He only told me because I ran a background check on him before I let him near the school and he didn't want me to be shocked."

Jenny could see Billy trying to have *that* conversation. "Well, he told me."

She left it at that. Anything else she said at this point would just further highlight the whatever-it-was that was going on between her and Billy.

Another pause. "Is something going on between you two?"

"Of course not."

How on earth could she entertain the notion of having a relationship with a man who'd been sentenced for public drunkenness? She was a responsible woman. She couldn't let Seth hang around someone who was a bad influence. Heavens, *she* shouldn't be hanging around with such a bad influence. Even if she really wanted to.

"He's spending a lot of time with Seth. Building the bike after school. I'm just checking. That's all."

"Uh-huh." She wasn't fooling Josey. "Listen, I'll start beating the bushes for more funding and you let me know if you have any other *questions* about Billy."

Jenny could hear the smile in Josey's voice. Part of her wanted to tell Josey all about the two kisses, about the way he brought her tea and got Seth to do chores, even at home. Part of her wanted to pump Josey for any and all information.

But a bigger part of her didn't. To talk about something made it real, and the whole thing—especially that kiss tonight—still had a dreamy feel to it. If Jenny told Josey, Josey might tell Jenny's mom, and the news that she was "involved" with Billy would filter its way through the school and the rez.

Even though it had been fourteen years since she'd blindly followed a boy over the edge of reason, everyone would say, *There goes that boy-crazy Jenny Wawasuck again. Some people never change.*

No. She'd worked too hard to become a respectable woman to let a couple of revelatory kisses muck up the works. Her first job was taking care of Seth. Her second job was guiding the TAPS girls into adulthood. Her third job was teaching. That was all she had room for in her life.

"Don't worry," she said with certainty. "I won't."

Ben paused when Josey's phone rang, but after she answered it, he sank the eight ball to win the round. Billy grunted in disgust. Normally, he could whip his brother at pool, but his game was off today.

And he knew why.

Then Josey sprinted—as fast as a woman in her condition could sprint—over to her and Ben's bedroom. What if it was Jenny? Was she calling her cousin to check up on him?

He felt ridiculous. What kind of man told a woman he was going to ask her out—later? It was nothing short of lame. But Jenny had a way of getting under his skin and muddling up his thinking.

Which probably explained what he was doing at his brother's place, playing pool instead of working on a bike. But it had been either this or hit a bar and get stupid, and Billy was done being stupid.

He hoped.

Once Josey was safely out of earshot, Ben started on him. "What's on your mind, bro?"

"What?"

Ben grinned at him. He smiled a lot more now than he used to. In fact, since he'd met Josey, he'd seemed happy. "You look lost in thought. It's a bit different from your usual seething."

Nothing like being the punch line in your own life. "Bobby give you that joke?"

"Take it easy. I'm just asking. If not as your brother, then as your financial partner."

Billy racked the balls. "Speaking of financials…"

"All safely invested. Been a little rough in this economy, but you're still firmly in the black. Why?"

Part of him wondered if he could just cash in some chips and cut a check to the school, specifically for Jenny's program. "How hard would it be to cash some out? Fifteen or twenty grand?"

Ben gave him a stricken look. "The financial penalties would be steep, man. I could move some around but it'd take me a few months. It'd be best to wait until next year—for tax purposes."

Damn, that was a long way off. All that money just sitting in the bank where he couldn't touch it. When Ben had told him about his most recent investment opportunities, he'd explained that the cash would be locked up tight for a while. Billy just hadn't realized how tight that would be.

He changed the subject—again. Sooner or later, Ben would catch on. "How's the remodel going?"

Now that Josey was expecting, they were making some changes to the huge, open space that was their loft home. Off the bedroom, walls that went all the way up to the ceiling now boxed in a baby's room.

Ben stared at him for a second before answering the question. "Good. On time and under budget." That was the thing Billy liked about Ben. Ben would let him dodge a conversation bullet, whereas Bobby would reload and come up firing. "How are things going at the school?"

"Okay, I guess. I think I scare the kids a little."

Ben broke, sinking a stripe. "You scare the hell out of everybody, dude."

Billy used to believe that. "Not everyone."

Ben missed his shot. "What?"

Damn it, he should have kept his mouth shut. Too late now. Because he didn't know what to say, he lined up a shot.

Ben waited until after he'd sunk in the four ball before starting in on him. "Who is she?"

Was there any way around this? Probably not. If Jenny wasn't talking to Josey right now, she'd talk to her later—Josey was supposed to be at the school in a couple of days. And Billy doubted that Josey wouldn't tell her husband that her cousin was messing around with his brother.

He gave it his best shot. "Bobby wants to auction me off, man. A bachelor auction."

Ben nodded, seemingly willing to let the "who" question slide. "I heard. Could raise a lot of money for the school."

Money that Jenny needed for the pregnant girls. Money that Don needed to keep the boys from getting the girls pregnant in the first place. Money that neither of them had, which meant that more kids would wind up screwing up their lives like Billy had.

He hadn't lied to Jenny. He wasn't a nice guy. If it had been any other woman in the world telling him she needed money, he probably wouldn't have even bothered to respond. But it wasn't any other woman. It was Jenny. He couldn't believe he was even considering this crazy plan to save her little program.

"So what you're saying is, you've got your eye on someone and being auctioned off to the highest bidder might trash your grand plans?"

That was his brother Ben, direct and to the point.

"Screw up my whole *life*. Bobby was talking about getting a big cable show. I don't wanna be a reality star. I didn't want to be a web star. I don't want any of this."

Ben rolled his eyes. "Seriously—that's what he told you?" When Billy gave him a confused look, Ben began to laugh. "That little jerk. Yes, he's working on a cable version, but Dad's going to be the focus—crazy Bruce Bolton and his three crazy sons. You won't be the only one on camera—hell, you probably will only be filmed when you're arguing with Dad or Bobby." He shook his head. "He was trying to get a rise out of you, brother."

"Why would he do that? Besides, you know, being Bobby."

Ben shot him a look. "Was there a camera nearby?"

At first, he was going to say no, but then he remembered—the camera Bobby had bolted to the wall of the shop. "Damn. Why does he do that?"

Ben shook his head, as if he couldn't quite get a handle on it himself. "He's got something to prove—at least, that's what Josey says. I guess he's got to prove it to us. Or to himself."

Billy wasn't sure he could believe that, but Ben was the straight shooter in the family. Why did Bobby have to prove anything? Yeah, he drove Billy nuts, but they were still brothers. He always had his brothers' backs. *Always.*

"Are you serious?"

Ben was always serious. "He didn't mention the real estate deal?"

"Just that he wanted to sell me to the highest bidder."

"Shoot, man. He's got this whole thing planned out—and you're a small part of it. Did he at least tell you that Josey thought the bachelor auction was a good idea?"

Being *a small part of it* didn't make Billy feel any better. "Just that she said I could say no. Which I did. I don't want anyone to buy me."

Anyone except Jenny. But he and Jenny didn't exist on camera. If Bobby were going to auction him off for the publicity, how would she buy him without being on camera? Hell, given the conversation they'd almost had this afternoon, how would she afford him at all?

"Buy yourself."

Billy's head snapped up so fast he might have sprained a neck muscle. "What?"

"Rig it." Ben grinned. "I know a woman who'd be willing to act as your proxy."

Billy blinked at his brother.

Josey walked over and took her seat on a stool. Billy noticed that she seemed more…thoughtful than she had before the phone call. For some reason, that made his ears burn. "What'd I miss?"

Ben kissed her on the cheek. His hand snaked around her back and rubbed. Then he put his other hand on her increasing belly and patted. Billy would have had to have been blind not to see the way Josey's face softened as she leaned into Ben's touch. But he wasn't blind. Watching that happy little family hurt so much that he turned his attention back to the pool table. Anything not to be reminded of what he didn't have.

"You're going to buy Billy at the auction," Ben announced, looking smug.

"I am?"

"She is?"

"You are. She is. That is, if you're willing to cover the cost. Bobby thinks you're worth a couple thousand. All of which would be tax deductible, of course."

Right. Because that was the most important part of this. What the hell was wrong with him that he was even considering agreeing to this madness?

It got worse. Josey shot him a look. "I'd be happy to give my winning bid to anyone you choose."

Billy slammed his pool cue on the table. He knew that Josey didn't like foul language, so he managed to keep the string of curse words in his head. That *had* to have been Jenny on the phone, or else someone had to have seen him kiss the hell out of her. Either way, Josey knew.

A fact that was hammered home when she added, "You know, Ben and I were thinking of having Seth over for a weekend—give Jenny a little parenting break. I'm sure we could coordinate the timing."

"Jenny?" Ben's jaw dropped as he stared at Billy, then at Josey. "Your *cousin* Jenny?"

Yup. There was no way around this mess. Only through it. He'd lost control of his own life again. "I'm only agreeing to this on *one* condition. Whatever I cost goes directly to Jenny's program."

"Deal." The speed at which Josey agreed let Billy know she'd been planning on that the whole time.

He felt tricked, but that was tempered by a secondary emotion—excitement. What if this actually worked?

"Wait—I have another condition. Bobby and his film crew aren't allowed to tail me when the winner cashes in the date night. Because that's what it is, right? A date? One whole night?"

"Jenny?" Ben asked again, not keeping up with the negotiations for possibly the first time in his life. "Jenny Wawasuck? And *you?*"

Josey looked worried. "If your brother catches wind of it…"

Yeah. If Bobby thought he could increase the number of hits he'd get, he'd start following Jenny around. And if he upset Jenny, Billy might not get his date.

"So don't tell him. Don't tell anyone." Ben seemed to have recovered a little. "Make it a surprise. If no one knows except the three of us, then it won't get out. We'll make sure Bobby doesn't follow you. You do the rest."

"Not even Jenny?" He asked this question of Josey, who appeared to think on it.

"A thoughtful surprise might be really nice. Heaven only knows she hasn't had enough surprises in her life." She spoke slowly, as if she wasn't sure that was the right answer. "No one's ever whisked her away for a—" she blushed "—a romantic night."

Billy wasn't sure, either. But Ben said, "Knowing Jenny, I bet if you told her you were going to plunk down a couple of grand, she'd throw a fit—even if it were for a good cause. She won't even let us help her out—there's no way in hell she'll let you do this without some serious grief."

Billy thought about it. He remembered how she'd tried to pay him back for the tea—and that had cost, what, three bucks? Ben was right. She'd threaten to feed him to the coyotes.

"Besides," Ben added, "women like it when you go the extra mile for them." He grinned at his wife. "I still have a few tricks up my sleeve."

Thoughtful. Was this what the world was coming to— Wild Bill Bolton debating romantic, thoughtful surprises? This would kill his reputation if it got out—or got on film.

"Fine. No one knows but us." But he was feeling greedy. He didn't want to wait three more weeks to see Jenny. But he couldn't do anything that would tip off Bobby.

Then it hit him. They were making good progress with the bike, him and Seth. They'd have to paint it—but that had to happen at the Crazy Horse shop. The school didn't have the setup for painting. "What about before then?"

Ben shook his head. "Man, you are *gone.*"

"What do you mean?" Josey asked.

"If we get the bike done soon enough, I could have them come into town—have Seth help me paint it. Could we all hang out here?"

The sly smile on Josey's face was all he needed. "I think we can reach an agreement on that."

A bonus day, and one guaranteed night with no classrooms, no kids, no shops and no damn cameras. He'd get one night with Jenny and she'd get the money she needed.

He could still say no. The bachelor auction would be

crawling with the kind of entitled society women he'd been avoiding ever since he'd earned his first million. Bobby would film the whole thing and maybe get his reality show and make Billy that much more famous. He *hated* being famous.

Being auctioned off was an assault on his dignity—and that was saying something. He could go back to what he'd been doing for years—building bikes day and night, trying not to look at how freaking happy his brother and sister-in-law were going to be with their new baby.

He could say no and go back to being left alone.

To being lonely.

One night...wasn't much of a guarantee that he wouldn't be lonelier after he finished the charity bike and didn't have an excuse, good or bad, to be out on the rez at the butt crack of dawn every morning.

Then he thought of the way Jenny stood before him, her hand on the thorn-covered rose tattooed over his heart, without a hint of fear in her eyes. He didn't expect one date to mean that Jenny would fall into bed with him. But given that last kiss...

He might be lonelier when it ended, but he was pretty sure someone, somewhere had once said something about it being better to have loved and lost than to have never loved at all.

One night with a woman like Jenny, a woman who was too good, too respectable for the likes of him.

He was in.

"She isn't afraid of me," Billy simply said.

Then he cleared the pool table.

Ten

Billy was waiting for them at school on Monday morning, his huge truck parked next to her spot. Jenny could see the extra cup of tea in his hand as she parked.

Was it wrong to be so thrilled that he'd brought her tea? Boy, she hoped not.

"Morning, kid." Billy nodded to the back of the truck. "Got some boxes for you today."

Seth grumbled. But he did so quietly, loading up his arms and trudging to the shop.

Jenny wasn't sure what would happen next. The last time she'd seen Billy, he'd kissed her, hard. She'd be lying if she said she didn't want him to do it again, but she wasn't entirely comfortable with the whole sneaking-around vibe. The problem with sneaking around was that, sooner or later, you got caught. She'd only been caught once and had spent years proving she was a responsible person. She had no desire to repeat the experience.

"Need to talk to you," Billy said in a tone of voice that made it pretty clear that he wasn't about to ravish her in a school parking lot. The sky was pinking overhead, giving him a warm, almost cuddly look.

"Oh?" She took her tea, not bothering to keep her touch on his fingertips light. Instead, she stood on her tiptoes and kissed the part of his cheek that wasn't covered with facial hair. "Everything okay?"

He didn't say anything for a moment, which made her nervous. Then his gaze darted behind her, and she heard Seth's plodding footsteps. "Yeah. About that…event we were discussing."

Was this biker code for date? "Yes?"

His words rushed out of him. "My brother wants to have a high-priced bachelor auction when we sell the bike. The funds would go to the school. So our *event* would have to wait until after the auction." His mouth snapped shut, and she saw him pull back.

Jenny felt herself blinking as she tried to process what he'd said. Bachelor. Auction.

"Bobby wants to sell you?"

Of all the ridiculous things she'd ever heard…the only thing that topped it was Billy agreeing to do it.

"Wasn't my idea."

That was a cop-out defense and they both knew it. Her event—her date—was going to take a backseat to some other woman buying him? "But you're going along with it."

They were silent as Seth came and went with the last box.

"Josey wants some of the kids—and your girls—to be there. I want you to come."

"Josey knows about this? But I talked to her a couple of days ago."

This explained why that woman had been so vague about additional funding for the school. She'd been holding out. Jenny was going to have words with her cousin.

Billy leaned forward. "It wasn't her fault." His voice was pitched low, even though Seth wasn't near. "I wanted you to hear about it from me."

There was something sexy about the way he said that. When had she gotten to the point where a man taking responsibility had become a turn-on?

"When?" It was cruel to ask her to watch someone else get him before she did.

"Three weeks."

Three whole weeks felt like a very long time to her. By then, the bike would be finished and she wouldn't see Billy first thing in the morning and last thing before she went home. But those three weeks would be like now—trying to have a conversation around Seth, without anyone recording it. Stolen hints of a relationship.

On the other hand, what was three weeks but another drop in the bucket? She found herself doing some quick math. She hadn't had a relationship since Seth had been three, when he'd started calling the last guy Jenny had been with "Daddy." Which had, predictably, freaked out the poor guy and sent him running for the hills. That had been the point when Jenny had realized her attempt to remain a typical teenager with a normal social life was hurting her son. That had been the point where she'd stopped dating.

She'd been eighteen then. Eleven years was a long time without sex. Far too long. What was three more weeks?

Then, like a bolt out of the blue, an idea struck Jenny. He was asking her to come to the auction, after all. Why not make the most of it? She had a little money saved up from back when the state had been paying the bills. True, she'd been hoping to save that for Seth's college, but she'd already been considering dipping into that to fund TAPS for a few more months. If she used that money to buy Billy, that was practically the same thing, right? The money would still go toward the program. And she'd have a chance to get Billy all to herself before their date.

She could make this work. She owned one dress that could blend in with high society—her bridesmaid's dress from Josey's wedding. It was a slinky, sleeveless pewter-gray gown with a cluster of rhinestones in the middle of her cleavage and a slit up the back—far sexier and fancier than anything else she had ever owned. And what's more, it had looked *good* on her. It had taken three trips to a tailor but combined with the heels, she'd looked surprisingly long and lean and, well, glamorous. More glamorous than she ever had before.

And where else would she wear such a fabulous dress? Certainly not to school, and not to the grocery store. No. The only other place in the world—or at least in South Dakota—where she could possibly wear this dress was to a charity bachelor's auction. And if she was going to go, she darned well wasn't going to sit around and watch someone else take Billy home. She wasn't going down without a fight.

He must have taken her silence wrong. "I'm on the clock, Jenny. If I don't get this bike done before the auction, I'm in a world of hurt. But I'm working on a way to see you before the auction. If we get the bike done, I'll be able to take some time off and we can do something. Just… be patient with me."

"I can't wait forever."

He gaped at her in surprise, which made her feel even more powerful. Yes, she wanted him and yes, she wasn't exactly in high demand right now. But she wasn't going to throw herself at a man, no matter how good his kisses were.

When he leaned forward this time, she responded in kind. So he was richer, bigger and infinitely more dangerous. They were still equals in this dance. Because that's what it was—a slow, exquisite dance of promise and hope.

"I promise you this, Jenny." She could hear the amusement in his voice, as if he liked it when she challenged him. But then his tone deepened, and heated goose bumps ran roughshod down her back as the scruff on his cheek rubbed against hers. His breath was warm on her ear, almost as if he'd touched her with his hand.

"Yes?" Her voice wavered, but she wasn't done dancing with him. Not by a long shot.

A deep, rumbling noise sprang out of his chest. If he'd been a big cat, it would have been a purr. As it was, it was something else—something much more sensual. Something that told her he'd keep his promise.

"I'll make it worth the wait."

The weeks until the auction passed at what felt like a snail's pace to Jenny. Every time Billy touched her, time slowed down. Which happened every day.

She brought him tea on the mornings he rode his bike. When he drove his truck, he had tea waiting for her. Their hands touched under the pretense of caffeinated beverages. In the afternoon, she'd head out to the shop after her TAPS meeting. Billy held to his word—when Jenny was in the shop, the hottest thing that happened was a few smoldering looks.

It was driving her insane. True, light touches and hot looks were far more interaction with the opposite sex than she'd had in a long time, but each day added to a frustration that became more and more physically painful. She tried to ignore the pressure. She'd done so without much problem for years now, so she didn't understand why it was harder this time. The motorcycle they'd be auctioning off took shape. One afternoon, wheels appeared on the bike. The next, handlebars and a seat. Finally, eight days before the Saturday night auction, the bike was finished, except for the paint.

When Jenny walked into the shop that Friday afternoon, Billy was on the phone with Seth hovering near him. When the boy saw her, he jumped up. "So, I got an A on that history test," he began, brandishing the paper. "Ms. Dunne says I'm getting an A this quarter."

"That's great, honey." And it was. But this sudden volunteering of information had her on high alert. She looked at Billy, who met her gaze with—was that a wink?

"And I think I aced that math test today," Seth went on as Billy continued to talk into his cell phone. It was the first time she'd seen him use one. "And Ms. Dunne says I pulled my science grade up to a B."

"Did she, now? That's great." Those were, hands down, the best grades Seth had gotten in a long time. Jenny paused to look at the bike.

"How do you paint it?" she asked, circling the silver-and-black thing. It was beautiful, in a way that she found slightly scary. After all, Seth had helped build it. Was it road worthy?

"And I already finished that book report that's due for English next Wednesday."

Jenny focused on her son. "Is that so? Okay, spill it. What's up?"

But Seth didn't say anything. He looked at her as though she were sentencing him to certain death.

Dear Lord, what had he done now? How big of a mess would this be? "Seth..."

As soon as she said it, Seth pointedly looked back at Billy. "You paint it," he said, answering the wrong question, "by taking it apart. I have specialized equipment at the shop. We have to do it there."

The tension in the air was something special. "And?"

"And I thought it'd be fun for the kid here to come down to the shop and see how the painting works, since he worked so hard to help me get it done on time."

She looked at Seth, who had puppy-dog eyes. "Can I, Mom? Please?"

"What's the catch?"

"No catch. But it's a long drive, so I asked Josey if you two could crash at their place Saturday night." Heat danced in his eyes, and Jenny felt her cheeks getting warm.

Boy, she hated the feeling that she was supposed to know what was going on and didn't.

"Us two?"

"Sure. I'd like you to come down." The casual way he said this didn't match his eyes at all. She saw nothing but want and need and desire in his gaze. "You can see the shop."

"And the bikes." Seth was hopping up and down again. "Billy said we could go look at all his bikes."

"Josey wants you to call her. You're supposed to use my phone." He held it out to her as if this whole thing were no big deal.

And maybe it wasn't supposed to be. She'd stayed over at Josey and Ben's modified warehouse mansion before.

But Billy was asking her—them—to come to the shop, to see his bikes. Maybe it wasn't supposed to be a big deal, but it felt huge.

Then he said, "Why don't you have a phone?"

She swallowed. The honest answer was that phones were far too expensive. The only slightly less honest, but still truthful answer was that reception on the rez was terrible on the best of days. She decided to hedge her bets. "Never needed one."

She took the phone, but was at a loss on how to make an actual call. Heck, she wasn't even sure how to turn the darn thing on. She'd used Josey's cell a few times, but this was a different one—sleek, silver and *very* expensive-looking. Billy stood and, without removing it from her hand, tapped until Josey's number appeared. Josey answered on the first ring. "Well?"

"What's going on?"

Josey laughed. "What's going on is that Billy wants to show you what he does when he's not in the school's shop."

"And what is that?"

"I suppose you'll have to see to find out. Come down for the day," Josey said.

Seth and Billy were hanging on her every word. They weren't even pretending to do something else.

"Well?" Josey asked, now sounding worried. "What do you want to do?"

Worst case, Jenny got to sleep in a big, soft bed for the night and eat a meal that someone else cooked and have someone else clean up afterward. Worst case, she got to hang out with her cousin. Worst case, Seth would learn a little more about how to build a bike.

Best case, though, was that she'd get to see what Billy Bolton was like when he wasn't working. He'd get to see what she was like when she wasn't being a teacher. He might even get to see her when she wasn't being a parent, first and foremost. Seth loved Billy's brother Ben—and he especially loved Ben's expensive gaming system.

Seth was still silently begging. Jenny locked gazes with Billy. Something in his eyes made her break out in goose bumps again—challenging her. She raised an eyebrow at him.

"What time should we get there?"

Eleven

"Dude, stop. You're making me dizzy."

Billy stopped pacing and turned to face Jack Roy, his painter. Normally, he liked Jack. Jack was about ten years older than he was and had worked for Billy's dad when Billy had been in high school. He smoked, drank, chased skirts and painted anything and everything he could get his hands on. But today, Billy didn't much care for Jack. The man sat on his stool, his hair slicked back under a red bandanna. His painter's coveralls were loosely knotted at his waist. The only thing covering his chest was a nearly see-through white tank top and a hemp necklace. He must be good-looking to women, because he was going to be auctioned off along with Billy in one week.

Billy didn't like it. What if Jenny did? So he grunted at Jack.

Jack laughed. "Seriously? You said this was some kid coming to watch. Why are your panties in a twist?"

"Watch your mouth," Billy shot out.

Jack looked Billy over. Billy had showered and cleaned up the edges of his beard. Hell, he'd even put on a little aftershave. A fact which did not go unnoticed by Jack.

"Hey, this kid—he wouldn't happen to have a mother, would he?" Jack threw up his hands. "Man, I've seen you go 'round with your old man enough. I got it. Kid and mom are off-limits."

Billy glared at him. "See to it." Which only got another laugh out of Jack.

Then, Billy saw the front door of Crazy Horse Choppers open up through the glass partition that separated the showroom from the shop floor. Cass, the receptionist, worked Saturdays and had gotten to be a pretty good saleslady. But otherwise, the place was deserted. The shop shut down at four-thirty on Friday and most everyone hit the bars. Hell, given that it was ten-thirty Saturday morning, half of his crew was probably still at a bar. The other half was sleeping it off.

Except on days like today. Jack had come in as a personal favor. Billy probably shouldn't kill him. "Be right back."

Cass was smiling at Jenny when Billy opened the door. Seth was doing that bunny-hop thing he did when he was excited. Billy felt himself grin at the boy. He remembered being that excited, once. Felt like a lifetime ago. "Hey, you found it."

Jenny's eyes were wide. Billy couldn't tell if she was as excited as her son or just plain old nervous.

Man, she looked *good*—not like a schoolmarm, not even like a mom. Hair flowing down her back, a pretty top and jeans that he knew would make her butt look amazing. She looked like she was far too good for him, but he didn't care. She looked like a woman—the woman he wanted.

"You gave good directions."

Cass made a small noise that almost qualified as a snort. Billy shot her a warning look. Between her and Jack, the whole shop would have the lowdown by Monday morning. Next week was going to be hell. And that was all *before* the auction. He wanted to be furious with Bobby for taking over his life, but then Jenny favored him with one of those small, challenging smiles, and he decided Monday didn't matter so much. "Come on back."

He couldn't help it. They were nowhere near a school and Bobby didn't film him when he wasn't at the school. So he put his hand on the small of her back as she passed him and didn't pull it away once she was through the door.

"Jenny, Seth, this is Jack Roy, my painter." Jack bowed, the rat fink.

"Nice to meet you," Jenny said. Then she looked at Billy and he realized he was growling. At Jack.

"Isn't this cool, Mom? See? Billy took it apart and now we're going to paint it!"

"Easy, kid. First, suit up." Jack tossed some coveralls at Seth. Then he looked at Jenny, held up a set of coveralls and waited.

"I'll just watch," Jenny said, not getting any closer.

"You'll have to stay in the waiting room. Too many fumes."

"Fumes? What about Seth?" Then Jack held up the extra mask. "Oh, okay. Well, then…have fun."

Billy walked her back to the door. "This will take a few hours. Will you be okay?" Man, he liked that smile on her. Warm and soft and sweet, but with a hint of tart challenge behind it. He liked it even more that she smiled at him and *not* at Jack. Then she touched his cheek and he almost forgot all about painting.

"I'll be fine."

"I'm coming over for dinner at Ben's," he added. "After we're done here."

He knew he couldn't rush the paint job. He never rushed a bike, because that's when mistakes happened, and as his brother Ben constantly pointed out, mistakes cost both time and money. But for the first time in a long time, he wanted to get done with the bike as fast as he could. For the first time in a stupid long time, he had plans that didn't involve welding.

Her fingers traced over the edge of his beard. He knew they had an audience, but he was powerless to do a damn thing about it. He wanted to stand there and look down into her eyes and not give a damn about what anyone else thought. Just him and her and this moment.

Then Jack whistled, Cass laughed and Seth said, "Ready!"

"Tonight," he said, feeling the pressure of her fingertips against his skin before she pulled away.

"It's a date" was all she said.

Jenny watched the three white-clad figures through the glass wall. As far as she could tell, no actual painting was occurring, but they were wearing masks and doing things, so she chose to assume that all was going well.

"You going to the auction?" Cass asked. Jenny tensed.

"Yes. You?"

She didn't know what else to say. Cass was the kind of hard-looking woman who fit in at a chopper shop. Cass wore a tank top and a leather vest and jeans that Jenny swore were acid-washed, and she could probably hold her own in a brawl.

By comparison, in the better of her two pairs of blue jeans and the cutest shirt she owned, a half-sleeve lilac top with big flowers outlined in embroidery and beads, she didn't feel like she belonged. Josey had gotten the top for Jenny last year on her birthday. It was only the second time she'd worn it. And she'd never been in a brawl. Heavens, she'd never even punched a person. That was not the sort of thing she did.

"Got my eye on someone," Cass said, staring extra hard through the glass.

This statement sent a spike of fear through Jenny. Surely this woman wasn't looking at Billy?

Then Cass laughed. "Don't worry, honey. We ain't after the same Bolton." She half patted, half slugged Jenny on the shoulder. Jenny managed to keep her balance in her one pair of fancy shoes—the satin pumps that went with her dress.

Should she ask which Bolton Cass was after? No—a certain measure of ignorance was, in fact, bliss. So she said, "That's good," as the front door opened and Cass went to attend to the customers.

Jenny sat in one of the big leather armchairs and kept an eye on the three figures. She couldn't tell which one was Billy and which one was Jack—they were both big men—but every so often, one white-clad figure would pause and turn his masked face in her direction.

Billy was keeping an eye on her. All she had to do was make it until tonight.

Five hours later, Jenny and Seth were riding up the freight elevator at Ben and Josey's. Jenny felt a little queasy, although she didn't think that was from the jerky elevator. No, the way Billy had peeled out of the lot on his bike after a hurried "I got something to do at home. I'll meet you there," had her nerves on edge.

Earlier, he'd said he was coming over, but had made no mention of *something he had to do*. This was supposed to be an almost date, wasn't it? That was the whole point, right? Well, how the heck could it be an almost date if he wasn't here?

The elevator lurched to a stop and Seth opened the doors. They'd been here enough that he knew what to do. Then he was out, running down the long aisle that divided Ben's warehouse into separate living quarters. "Josey! Ben! I painted a bike today!"

Ben's head popped out of the room he was converting into a nursery for the baby. The room had mint-green walls and doors. In Jenny's opinion, Ben hadn't been overly emotional about the baby, due in four months. But he was putting a lot of time into that room, getting it just right.

"Hey, come tell me what you think of this bookcase here," he said.

Jenny shook her head as she followed him into the nursery. Men. *Boltons*. Not so good with emotions, better with tools. Maybe Ben didn't gush. But he was here, working on behalf of the baby and Josey.

Was it wrong to want someone to take care of her, too?

She pushed the selfish thought away. She took care of herself. That had always been enough before. Before she'd met Billy.

Ben was waiting. Jenny studied the bookshelf. "Looks good." He nodded his approval and asked Seth to help him with something.

Josey appeared. "How was the shop?"

"Okay. Met Jack, the painter."

Josey's eyes wrinkled up with a deep smile. "Where's Billy?"

"He said he had something to do at home and he'd meet us here." This pronouncement was met with a frown, but Jenny didn't want to dwell on how this evening could go wrong. So she patted Josey's growing belly. "Any kicks yet?"

"Maybe." Josey beamed as she moved Jenny's hand below her belly button. "You're the expert here. You tell me."

Another pang of loss hit Jenny as she felt the tiniest of flutters. Fifteen years ago, she hadn't even known she was pregnant until those little flutters got stronger, to the point that Seth was karate-chopping her and she was forced to admit that it wasn't just gas and she wasn't just gaining a little weight. What had come after that had been sheer panic at telling her mom, then hope that Ricky would marry her and they'd live happily ever after. When that didn't happen, well, her world had kind of fallen apart.

At no point had she ever been able to enjoy being pregnant, to take the time to marvel at the gift of life she was creating. Years had passed before she got over not only the loss of Ricky, but also the loss of her carefree teenaged years. All because she'd lost her head over a bad boy. Well, maybe Ricky hadn't been all bad, but he certainly hadn't been good. Not as good as she'd tried to be ever since, as if she could make up for her mistakes.

Jenny was thrilled for Josey, she really was. But moments like this—Ben building a nursery by hand, Josey feeling the butterfly flutters—these were the moments she'd never had and probably never would. She couldn't even pull off an almost date. How was she supposed to settle down and take another crack at happily ever after?

"Definitely kicking," she said with a grin to Josey, trying to put her worries aside. "Give Sweet Pea here a few months. Remember how Seth kicked me so hard he rolled me over in bed once?"

Josey's eyes widened. She'd always thought that was a funny story, but now, she looked mildly terrified. "Yeah…"

Then she heard the freight elevator clanking, and her back stiffened. It had to be Billy. Part of her wanted to rush out and greet him. This was an almost date, after all. Wouldn't it be lovely to act like it?

But something held her back, and that something was the way he'd roared off after they had finished at the shop. She tried to tell herself that she was playing it cool, but that lie didn't hide the fact that she was more than a little unsure of what was going to happen next.

Josey went out first and said, "Oh!" in the tone of voice

that made it clear that the man outside wasn't what she'd been expecting.

Jenny tried not to rush out to see him, but she did walk a little quicker than normal. The first thing she noticed was the way Billy was standing. His feet were spread shoulder-length apart and his head was down. He looked like he could plow his way through a bar full of the baddest of bikers without getting a scratch on him.

She'd seen that look before, at Josey's wedding. Then, she'd thought he was pissed off at the world, a dangerous man to be avoided. Now, however, she saw something else. He didn't like that everyone had noticed him, and he liked it less that Josey had commented in surprise.

Then Jenny looked again, and saw why. Billy was wearing a pair of dark-washed jeans that looked expensive, instead of merely old and broken in. He had on another T-shirt, but this one was sea-foam green, with a texture to the fabric and a V at the neck. These things weren't so far beyond his normal attire, but the close-cut blazer he'd thrown on top of it all? The high shine to the shoes—that were not biker boots? The way his hair had been combed—but not pulled back into a ponytail? He was hot. Movie-star *hot*.

The heat that flashed down Jenny's back when Billy looked up and their gazes met was so fierce that it left her with an agonizing case of goose bumps. He'd gone home to change for *her*. And she appreciated the effort. Boy, did she appreciate it.

Then she saw the two small boxes tucked under one of his arms—one was a plain brown, the other had a bow on it. He noticed her looking.

"I had to go pick these up for you guys." He handed the plain one to Seth and the one with the bow to her.

"Presents? Awesome!" Seth snatched his up and began prying it open.

Jenny took the box much the same way she took her tea from him. Her fingers skimmed over the top of his, shimmering heat filling the air around them. It felt different this time. Everyone was watching them—and everyone knew what was going on.

"You didn't have to get us presents."

"A phone!" Seth yelled, snapping her out of her trance. "You got us phones? Man, that is so cool!"

"You got us phones?" The first thing she thought was, *How much did this cost?* Because it was one of those slick phones, just like Billy had. It wasn't just a phone. It was a sign that he had the money to walk right out and buy not one, but two of them.

"You need one." Then he blushed. "To call Josey," he added.

Behind them, Seth and Ben were talking about phone this and app that, but Jenny ignored them. After Bobby stopped filming at the school at the end of this week, Billy wouldn't be out there every morning and every night. However small and stolen the time they'd had in the past few weeks had been, it was all going to come to a crashing halt in a matter of days.

And he'd bought her a phone. No matter what he said, she knew it wasn't to call Josey. It was to call him. He wanted to keep talking to her.

It was the most thoughtful thing a man had ever done for her.

If they were alone, she'd kiss him. She'd kiss him long and hard, then she'd kiss him some more, hoping and praying the kiss led to something more, something selfish, something good.

But they weren't alone and her reality was unavoidable.

"I can't pay you back right now." Not when she was hording her precious few dollars to buy him at auction.

"You aren't paying me back at all. The plan is good for

a year. The kid's going to need a phone when he goes off the rez to high school next year, anyway. He earned it."

She wanted to protest—he couldn't spend this much money on *her*. Then Seth hit him midchest, a full-body hug-slash-tackle. "Thank you, thank you, thank you! This is *so* awesome!"

Billy awkwardly patted Seth on the head. "You're welcome, kid. Anytime you want to come back to the shop, give me a call. Had the guy put all the numbers in there."

Seth disengaged and started hopping. "Really? Man, that is *so* cool!"

Ben grinned over Seth's head. "Easy, kiddo. Come pick out what you want to drink for dinner—root beer or orange soda?" He and Josey led Seth away.

An awkward silence settled between Jenny and Billy. She needed to say something, but she was at a loss. No one had ever bought her such an extravagant gift, for that's what it was—extravagant. She knew there were cheaper phones on the market. She'd priced them. She still couldn't afford them, but she'd priced them.

"You didn't have to get me a phone." She realized she hadn't even opened her box yet.

"You don't like it." His blush deepened.

She was in danger of insulting him—again. So, even though it went against her financial principles, she stepped into him. "That's not it," she said, dropping her voice. "It's the most thoughtful thing anyone's ever given me." She stood on her tiptoes, put the hand without the box in it on his chest to balance herself and placed a kiss on his cheek, right above his beard. "Thank you."

One arm snaked around her waist and pulled her in tight, while his other hand captured hers and held it against his chest, right over his heart. The long, hard planes of his chest pressed against her front—muscles so firm they were almost unforgiving. But the way his hands held her body with that much gentleness? Her knees went weak.

A low rumble rose out of him, and the vibrations she felt as much as heard had such a sexual undertone that she wanted to do a whole lot more than kiss him. Heat flooded her belly.

"You look really pretty today."

All that heat pooled lower and she felt her hips shift against him. The pupils of his eyes widened in a look of pure desire. He leaned forward, his gaze glued to her lips.

Kiss me and make it worth it, she thought.

Then her box rang. "Mom?" Seth called out from the other side of the warehouse. "Are you going to answer it? Mom?"

A look of resignation blocked out the desire on Billy's face. But the amazing thing was, he didn't get mad or grumble about stupid kids or act like Seth's presence was a deal-breaker. Instead, he gave her a tiny smile and a quick squeeze around the waist and said, "We aren't done here," as he let her go.

"Better not be" was all she could say.

Then she answered the phone.

Twelve

Dinner took forever. Two forevers, by the time they ate dessert. Billy had to settle for sitting across from Jenny. The food was good, so there was that, but still, by the time Jenny made Seth carry in his dishes and Ben suggested they all play a game of pool, Billy was on the verge of punching something.

But Jenny smiled and blushed and said, "That would be fun," while she looked at him with those big eyes.

"Sounds good," he offered.

So that's how he found himself playing pool with Jenny against Ben and Seth while Josey sat and watched.

And Jenny was terrible. The only saving grace was that Seth was even worse, so the game was mostly Billy and Ben playing against each other. Which was fine, except Billy could do that anytime he wanted. And it wasn't how he wanted to spend his time with Jenny.

Luckily, his little brother wasn't stupid. After Ben sank the eight ball, he said, "Seth, did I tell you we got the newest 'Call of Duty'?"

"No way! Mom, can we play?"

Jenny got that look on her face that made it pretty clear

that, normally, she wouldn't exactly endorse a little warfare gaming. But she said, "I guess. But only for a little bit— you still have to go to bed at a reasonable hour."

Not that Seth heard that last part. He was already sprinting toward the TV room, Ben trailing him.

Josey sat on her stool for a bit before she said, "Well, I'm tired." She rubbed her back for emphasis. "Think I'll put the dishes in the dishwasher and go to bed."

"Need some help?"

Billy couldn't believe his ears. Had Jenny just offered to bail? When they were this close to not having anyone around?

But Josey quickly said, "No, I've got it. You have fun."

The women shared one of those feminine looks, and then, *finally,* he and Jenny were alone.

"We don't have to play pool, if you don't want."

Her cheeks pinked up real pretty. "I'm not that good…."

"You're holding your stick wrong." Her eyes flashed, but before she could snap off a smart response, he was behind her. "Here. I'll show you."

He angled her body, not bothering to keep any distance between them. He'd been waiting all day—all week—for this moment. No school, no cameras and no family. At least, not within line of sight.

Her body tensed against him. He moved her hair out of the way, giving him full access to her neck and ear. "I won't do anything you don't want me to, Jenny." Because he felt he had to prove to at least one of them that he wasn't lying, he leaned past her and picked up her cue. "Don't know why you loop your index finger over the cue. You're supposed to let it rest on your hand like this."

She hadn't said anything, and she continued not saying anything as he bent her forward, lined the cue up on her hand and guided her through a shot.

His thinking was blurring. The feeling of her pressed

against him was diverting all the blood from his brain to other parts—parts that were now straining behind his belt, against her backside. If he were a respectable man, he'd compliment her on that shot, maybe offer another tip on how to improve her aim and, most important, step away from her.

Too bad he had never been respectable.

He slid one hand around her waist under the swell of her breasts and pulled her in even tighter.

"I don't think you're playing fair," she said, her voice low and sultry.

"Never said I would."

She leaned back and ran her hand through his hair. "Your brother is in the next room."

He couldn't help it. He slid his hand up a few inches and took her breast in his palm.

She exhaled, her warm breath pulling him in closer. One taste, he thought as he dipped his head.

When their lips met, her body arched into his. Her nipple went rock-hard under his touch and his body responded in kind. Had he ever wanted a woman this badly? Was there anything he wouldn't do for her? Right now, with her soft curves melting into him, her teeth skimming his lips—sweet, merciful heaven, she was going to bring him to his knees.

She spun in his arms, which made everything better and worse at the same time. He picked her up and set her on the pool table. Her legs fell open. So it wasn't his fault that he had to step between them, and it wasn't his fault that he had to snake his hand back below her bottom to keep her from losing her balance and sprawling across the pool table. But it was a little bit his fault that he cupped her bottom and pulled her warm center toward him, and it was a whole hell of a lot his fault that he leaned into her, his full-on erection rubbing against her through two layers of denim.

Her head fell back as he ground against her, a low moan humming on her lips. Man, he had her right where he wanted her, and by the way she was digging her nails into his back, it was the same place she wanted to be.

"Jenny," he groaned. "Tell me what you want."

Even through his muddled thinking, he knew he'd promised her that he wouldn't do anything she didn't want him to. And that was the sort of promise a man kept, no matter what.

"I—"

"Oh, man! No fair!"

At the sound of Seth's whine from the TV room they both shrank back. How hard up was he? So hard up that he'd almost done unspeakable things on his brother's pool table.

Eyes wide, Jenny was obviously coming to the same conclusion. She pushed him back. Not away, but back. "Is this a date?"

He felt the corner of his mouth curl up. "No." What he wouldn't give for a date.

"No?"

He leaned forward so he could feel the pressure of her hands on his chest. "If this were a date, we'd be alone and I'd lay you out on this pool table, strip those jeans off you and I wouldn't stop until you screamed my name." It sounded so good that he was having a little trouble remembering why he didn't go ahead and do it now.

"Again," Seth demanded in the distance.

"You're on, kid," Ben replied.

Oh, yeah. This wasn't a date because they weren't alone. It came down to that.

"When are we going to have a date, Billy?" She leaned

up, her voice low as she went from holding him back to rubbing his chest.

"After the bachelor auction." One week. One week that might break him.

A look of doubt flashed over her face. "I don't know if I can wait that long."

He folded her into his arms. "I'll make it worth it," he promised again. Man, he hoped he was doing the right thing, planning their first date as a surprise.

She pushed him back and, with the sounds of the video game echoing behind them, he had no choice but to step away.

"What do we do until then?"

Right. What did they do if they weren't having sex? "Uh…"

What did people do on dates? It had been such a long time since he'd had a date—a real date, not getting drunk in a bar. Actually, it had been a long time since he'd done even that.

Then he looked down and saw the concentration on her face. For the first time, he found himself wondering how long it had been for her.

He wanted to make this count.

She took a deep breath and appeared to get more control over herself than he was currently feeling. "We could watch a movie. Lots of people do that."

Yeah, he remembered that. He'd gone with Ashley to the movies in high school. He didn't remember watching any films…no, what he remembered was getting in a hell of a lot of trouble in the dark.

Yeah—no cameras hovering around, no kids barging in on them. He'd been waiting for this for weeks. He was going to make the most of this. Bring on the darkness.

Except…Jenny wasn't the kind of woman who normally let things get heavy the moment the lights dimmed. He'd be lucky if she didn't haul off and smack him, because keeping his hands off of her was going to be one hell of a challenge.

Damn. He was going to have to work harder on being good enough for her.

"Okay. A movie."

Her eyes lit up. She was killing him.

"I'll send Seth to bed."

Seth went to bed grumbling, but Jenny didn't care. It was ten o'clock. Ben had taken far less convincing. All he'd said was, "Josey go to bed already?" Then he'd winked and left them alone.

She sat on the couch as Billy flipped through the movies available through Josey's television. Jenny's stomach was nervous. At this point, she didn't care what they watched. Just so long as he picked something and turned off the lights.

After that kiss on the pool table, she didn't know what to expect. The two of them, alone in the dark…God, she wanted another kiss like that—but…*but*…

But a man like Billy, who was rough and tumble and had just threatened to strip her pants off of her and do horrible, terrible, *wonderful* things to her…what would stop him from doing that now? What would stop *her* from stopping *him*?

She was a respectable, *responsible* woman now, by God. She did not lose her head over bad boys anymore. Even if they were men like Billy.

He started a movie and settled beside her on the couch. He slid his arm around her shoulder and pulled her in. "Feel like I'm a teenager again," he whispered.

"I know what you mean."

There was something old-school about this. Not that she knew firsthand—she'd never had much trouble climbing out her bedroom window and running wild. But all this sneaking around was probably something normal teenagers did all the time.

She couldn't help but remember that sneaking always led to getting caught. She didn't want to get caught again. She didn't want to throw away everything she'd worked so hard to become. She wasn't the same girl who threw caution to the wind because of an irresistible bad boy.

Which was all well and good except for one small thing: she *wanted* Billy in a way that had nothing to do with sneaking around or immature fumbling.

God, this contradiction was going to drive her crazy.

Billy didn't say anything as the movie started up, but once they hit a stretch of dialogue, he leaned down and brushed his lips against her forehead. "I want to see you after I'm done with the build at the school."

"You had mentioned a date after the auction." She felt good under his arm. His chest—so broad—was warm and surprisingly comfortable. She nuzzled in deeper.

"More than that."

He tilted her head up so he could capture her lips again.

Even now, the heat that pooled between her legs made thinking difficult. As Billy's fingertips brushed over her breasts again, his movements steady and sure and—above all else—confident, the desire that gripped her went way beyond what she'd experienced as a teen. This wasn't wanting sex for the sake of having sex—this was more. She wanted Billy. She was starting to think she needed him.

His hand slipped lower, over the front of her jeans. Then his hand was against the part of her that hurt for him the most. "Do you want this?"

He pressed—with exquisite precision, he simply pressed against her.

Jenny's body bucked against his hand—his finger—his fingertip and the pressure he was using to control her. Because she wanted to give up control. She wanted to give up everything—everything she'd worked so hard for, everything she'd worked so hard to be. A good mother, a good teacher, a good daughter—a responsible adult who did the right thing. None of that mattered. The only thing that mattered was him touching her.

Billy shifted the pressure and she shook in his arms. He only held her tighter. "Tell me you want this, Jenny."

His voice was a direct order, one that threatened to swamp her.

"Yes."

She didn't know if she'd thought it or said it when he shifted against her again. The climax whipped her body against his, but he didn't lose his grip as she rode the wave.

"Woman," he said as he buried his face in her neck, his teeth skimming her skin.

She wanted more. One touch—one *single* touch didn't make up for the past eleven years. She needed more. She needed *him*.

"I'm not too good at this relationship thing." His voice was so low and deep that its vibrations sent another shock of pleasure through her.

She grinned, although he probably couldn't see it in the dark. "I'm out of practice, too."

"I want to try. With you."

She didn't say anything. She didn't have to.

She just kissed him.

One moment, Jenny was snuggling against a warm, hard body while she pleasantly drifted through a hazy sleep.

The next, her eyes snapped open in a panic. Seth was standing over her—her and Billy. Asleep. On the couch. Sweet merciful heaven, she was on top of Billy, one of her legs draped over Billy's thigh. Were they dressed? Yes. Thank God for small favors.

"Hey...guys."

Seth had a funny look on his face. She jolted and tried to sit up, but Billy's arms didn't fall away from her. If anything, he tightened his grip. That was when she realized his hand was in the space between her top and her waistband. Caressing her bare back.

In front of her son.

The panic that hit her was so strong she could taste it in the back of her mouth. "Seth! Um, we were, um, we were— How did you sleep? Do you want some breakfast?" She couldn't tell if her hardwired Mom instincts were a good thing or not.

Seth didn't say anything. He kept on staring. Behind him, the TV was a huge wall of blue screen. They must have fallen asleep before the movie ended, before things had gone too far.

"Kid," Billy said. Jenny's gaze snapped back on him. His eyes were still closed, and he hadn't let go of her yet, but he was at least a little awake. "Don't you know not to wake a man up before the coffee's ready?"

Then the weirdest thing happened. Seth looked sheepish and said, "Sorry."

"Go check." The order was anything but subtle, but then Billy added, "After I get going, I'll show you my bikes."

Seth stared at them with undisguised suspicion before he said, "Okay." At least the kitchen was four rooms away. It would take the boy some time to get there.

Jenny tried to sit up again, but Billy kept his hold on her. "Morning, beautiful," he said, his eyes still closed. He pushed her up to his lips and took a quick kiss. "I like waking up with you."

Part of her wanted to do nothing more than snuggle back down into his arms and maybe see where the morning went. But that part was overridden by panic.

And the worst part was, she wasn't sure why she was panicking so badly. So Seth had caught her and Billy together. They were both still fully dressed and hadn't even been kissing. If she and Billy were going to keep seeing each other—and that did seem like the plan—then sooner or later Seth would put one and one together.

But she wasn't ready for that first thing on a Sunday morning. Heck, she wasn't sure when she'd be ready. For too long, her life had been about her son. To do something as selfish as spend some time with a man—with Billy— felt foreign.

With a squeeze that bordered on crushing, Billy hugged her. "He'll be fine," he said as they sat up, almost as if he'd been reading her mind.

"But—"

She didn't get the chance to freak out, though. From the other side of the apartment, she heard Ben's voice, then Josey's. The rest of the house was up.

He took her hand, kissed her cheek and whispered, "Only six more days."

Six days until the bachelor auction. And after that? A real date.

How was she ever going to make it?

Thirteen

Six of the longest days of Jenny's life had finally come and gone. She'd seen Billy only for the first three. He and Seth had reassembled the bike on Monday at the school, then Bobby had spent the next two days finishing his filming.

In other words, even though she'd seen Billy for three days, she hadn't gotten to really talk to him. He'd kissed her on the cheek when he'd given her the ticket for the event—the ticket that said Admission: $100. When she'd protested, he'd cut her off with a look. "I want you there" was all he'd said. Who was she to argue with that? Besides, she couldn't have afforded to pay him back even if she'd wanted to. Not if she had a hope of buying him.

The two school days without Billy in the morning and Billy in the evening were even longer. However, the Saturday of the bachelor auction flew by so fast it left her dizzy. Before she knew it, her mom had curled her hair and she'd shimmied into her bridesmaid's dress and had loaded up Seth, several of his classmates and a half-dozen of her TAPS girls in the school van, along with Josey's mom, Sandra, and was barreling toward the reception center in Rapid City.

In the small purse that Jenny had clutched to her chest was $743 dollars—all of the money she had left from what the state of South Dakota had paid her to run TAPS. She had no idea what Billy would go for, but it was the best she could do. She had to hope it would be enough.

The kids were all excited, nervously chattering and messing around with the pretied bow ties and white shirts that Josey had delivered to the school. Josey wanted them to help with registration, so everyone would have the chance to meet the kids their money would be helping. And everyone was, well, everyone. Josey had run down a preliminary guest list with her. Half the city council was on that list. So were a few starlets that Bobby had sweet-talked into showing up, no doubt with promises of internet stardom. A lot of the names Jenny hadn't known, but Josey had. Wives and daughters of industry titans from South Dakota, Wyoming and parts of Montana. Heavens, there were even a few women ranchers attending. The whole thing was crazy.

Even Sandra seemed to crackle with a nervous energy. "A bachelor auction! Did you ever think we'd see the day?"

"No," Jenny had to admit.

Sandra gave her an odd look out of the corner of her eye. "Nervous, dear?"

Jenny forced herself to breathe in and out. "Hoping to make it through the evening without something going wrong." Which was true. That was a concern. Just not her primary one. She realized she was fluffing her hair again, which was probably not helping her beachy waves stay very beachy. She put her hands in her lap.

"I can handle the children." As if to illustrate this statement, Sandra looked in the rearview mirror and shouted, "Randy, where do your hands belong?"

"To myself" came the sheepish reply from the rear of the van.

"See?" Sandra actually reached over and patted Jenny on the arm. "You have fun tonight. I've got this covered." Jenny swore Sandra winked at her. "Got more than a few tricks up my sleeve."

Fun? Was fun an option tonight? Heck, she hadn't been this nervous at Josey's wedding, and she'd been so distraught there she'd almost thrown up before she'd walked down the aisle. That had been more about remembering to smile in front of a huge crowd while simultaneously trying not to step on the hem of her dress.

This was different. This was the very real possibility of seeing the man she wanted to take home going home with someone else. Billy had promised her a date. How would she watch him leave with another woman?

Well, she sort of knew the answer to that one. Not well. Not well at all.

Soon enough, the van was pulling up in front of the reception hall. Although the auction didn't start for another hour and a half, the place was already humming with activity. Jenny recognized the camera crew from the school, but they weren't the only ones with cameras running around. She counted four different local news vans, all setting up to do live feeds for the ten o'clock news. And because of the starlets, Bobby had even rolled out a red carpet. The highest of South Dakota's high society was strutting down the catwalk while photographers snapped shots. The whole thing was completely insane—and entirely out of her league.

Wearing a tux that fit him like a second skin, Bobby left his post on the red carpet, where he'd been glad-handing all the guests, and came to greet them. The kids crowded around and Bobby turned on the charm. "Okay, troops, come with me!"

Avoiding the cameras, he herded the whole crew inside. Within ten minutes he had them practicing greetings for the people who'd be keeping their school in the black for the foreseeable future. Then Bobby snagged Seth and had him helping backstage.

Jenny tried to relax, but it wasn't easy. Bobby was being his normal, irritating self—telling her she was in the way here—no, still in the way over there. Josey came by, but was too busy dealing with last-minute credit-card issues to talk Jenny down from the edge. Even Sandra disappeared. She was giving a short welcome speech and had to go practice.

Keeping an eye on the kids, Jenny looked for Billy. Bobby wasn't hard to miss, and she caught sight of Ben ushering various men backstage—including Don Two Eagles and Jack Roy.

But no Billy.

Bobby reappeared and hustled her over to a table set slightly off from the rest of the crowd. "Darned shame you can't be on camera," he said with that used-car-salesman smile of his. "You look amazing tonight."

Jenny waited for the demand that she do something, or a jerky plea for assistance—but nothing.

Well, that was…odd. If she didn't know any better, she'd say that Bobby Bolton had paid her a compliment. "Thank you. This is, um, impressive. You pulled this off!"

Bobby's smile deepened and for a moment, he looked more…real, somehow. "Thanks, Jenny. I hope we make a ton of money for the school tonight."

Then he looked over her shoulder and was gone, back to schmoozing someone more important than she was.

The room filled. Women in slinky black dresses, in dark business suits, in sequined numbers that were better suited to Miss America than anything else—suddenly, the room was *filled.* The cash bar in one corner was doing a booming business as an excited hum filled the air.

Jenny eyed her potential competition, her stomach sinking. A lot of the women looked smooth and elegant and effortless, like this was just another Saturday night. Jenny had taken a literature class when she'd gone back to school to get her teaching degree, and a line from a play she thought was Shakespeare came back to her. These women—they had a lean and hungry look about them, like they were going to pounce on the first hunk they saw and quite possibly rip him to shreds.

She didn't stand a chance.

Then Cass, the Crazy Horse receptionist, came and sat by her. Jenny almost hadn't recognized her. Cass had clearly been to a salon. Her hair was swooped up into an elegant French twist, and she was wearing an honest-to-goodness ball gown. "Cass! Wow!"

Cass winked, and underneath the professional makeup application, Jenny saw the same sparkling smile. "Hope you get your man, honey."

That made two of them. "You, too."

Cass grinned and filled the rest of their time with a running commentary on the various women she knew in the crowd. The statuesque blonde had ordered a bike for her husband three years ago, but they'd divorced since then. That woman with the bright white hair and the too-tight face? Her family owned a trust company.

The more Cass shared, the more worried Jenny got. These women weren't just rich—they were *really* rich. The lights dimmed and a spotlight lit up the stage. In front of a red-velvet curtain sat the bike that Seth had helped build. Bobby Bolton came out and the crowd applauded. He made some opening remarks in that smooth tone of voice about the men that would soon be for sale— "For the night, ladies!" He then introduced Sandra, who spoke for ten minutes about the school and the children and what the proceeds of the auction would go toward.

Jenny was surprised at the emphasis Sandra put on after-school programs—hers and the one Don wanted to start for the boys. Although the crowd remained polite, Jenny could sense the women getting restless. The teacher in her wanted to shush them, but she forced herself to be still.

Then Sandra was done, Bobby was back on stage, and the auction began. Bobby introduced everyone, but he'd brought in a real auctioneer to do the actual selling.

Jenny didn't know any of the men who went first. After the gavel fell the first few times, the only thing she was certain about was that she didn't have enough money. A guy with a slicked-back ponytail, a tie and a leather jacket oh-so-casually thrown over his shoulder went for nine hundred dollars. Jack Roy went for more than one thousand. Heavens, Don Two Eagles went for a healthy six hundred.

Then Bobby said, "Ladies, a true diamond in the rough—Bruce Bolton!" and the crowd went wild. Jenny had only met the senior Bolton once, at the wedding where he'd mostly stayed by the bar with a group of equally crusty-looking bikers. Josey didn't like him much and Jenny had gotten the feeling that Ben didn't exactly get along with his father.

Bruce Bolton trotted out on stage, looking for all the world like Hulk Hogan in a tux, only with less hair. The man was eating up the catcalls from the audience. He posed and preened while Bobby and the auctioneer cracked jokes about Bruce's "staying power."

Luckily, the bidding started. Jenny was shocked when Cass bid the first fifty dollars, and more shocked as she kept right on bidding, blowing all other hopefuls out of the water. She finally got her man for a cool $1,850.

"You bought Bruce?" Jenny couldn't help but whisper even as Cass smacked the tabletop in victory.

"That man's been bossing me around for years." Cass's smile was nothing short of wicked. "'Bout time that particular shoe was on the other foot."

Jenny decided it was best not to ask what, exactly, Cass meant and was thankful when she left to claim her prize.

The rest of the evening passed in a blur of good-looking men, insane bids and suggestive innuendo. Some of the guys from the rez—guys Jenny knew—brought in a pretty penny.

She tried to be happy at the huge dollar amounts being raised—all of this money was going to the school, to the TAPS program. They had to be nearing thirty-five thousand, at least—and they hadn't even gotten to the bike. This was wonderful. This was great.

She was on the verge of tears.

Finally, the end was near. She knew this not because she was keeping count of the number of hot men who'd paraded across the stage, but because Bobby auctioned himself off. He winked, blew kisses and waggled his eyebrows like a true lothario as the numbers went up and up.

Then the gavel fell. Jenny craned her neck around and spotted the busty redhead who was celebrating her victory in a sloshed way as the gavel fell. Nearly five thousand dollars.

Holy cow. Before the hugeness of that number could truly register, though, Bobby took the microphone. "And now, ladies, the moment we've all been waiting for—the man of the hour, 'Wild' Billy Bolton!"

Except the man who walked out on stage wasn't Billy—not the Billy she knew, anyway. Oh, he was tall and broad, and his hair was the same golden brown, but that's where the resemblance ended. This man had neatly cropped hair that sported a hint of wave. This man wore no beard, which made his strong jaw that much stronger. True, he was in a close-cut gray suit and not a tux—he didn't have on a tie, just a white button-up shirt with the top two buttons undone. He walked out on stage, paused, pivoted—and looked directly at her. The glare—for that's what it was—was white-hot, but she wasn't scared of it, nor of him.

Jenny wasn't sure if she was breathing or not. Billy looked ferocious, but she could see underneath the fury that he was unsure about this whole thing. That meanness was the cover he hid behind. Everyone else probably saw a brutal man, but she saw someone else. The man she wanted.

Bobby, darn his hide, opened the bidding up at five hundred dollars. Jenny knew she didn't have a prayer, but she held up her paddle anyway. So did half the room.

The bidding quickly left her in the dust. A thousand, two thousand—the number grew faster than Seth's shoe size. The auctioneer had abandoned the fifty-dollar increments he'd used for everyone else and was going up by two hundred dollars a shot. Even so, the bidding hit five thousand within five minutes, and at least four women were still in the running.

How ridiculous was she? Ridiculous enough to think she and her meager little $743 had a shot in heck of winning this auction. She almost wished Cass had come back to the table so that her saucy attitude would distract Jenny from her misery.

Billy seemed almost as miserable. He'd been standing up there for a long time, looking uncomfortable. For his sake, Jenny wanted the bidding to end so he could get off the stage.

Six thousand dollars came and went. The only consolation Jenny had was that another woman dropped out. Although she knew it was pouring salt into the wound, Jenny tried to see who the remaining three bidders were.

One was a raven-haired stunner in one of those slinky black dresses; the other was petite and curvy, with big blond hair. Jenny couldn't spot the third woman, but the auctioneer kept mentioning three numbers as the bids went up and up and up.

She wouldn't have thought it possible, but her hopes sank even further. She knew that if she'd bought Billy, she would have finally, *finally* broken her decades-long drought. She wouldn't have had to wait for another date— wait for the cameras to stop and the stars to align and the world to be perfect, because it already would have been. She would have gotten into his bed and stayed until she'd screamed in pleasure. She would have gone to sleep in his arms and woken up there, without a teenager standing over them. It would have been selfish and naughty and very, very good.

She eyed the two women she could see. Instead, Billy might be doing those things with one of them. She tried to hold on to the idea that he wouldn't sleep around at the drop of a hat, not when he was already involved with her, but she couldn't compete with those women and, really, how involved were they? Was Billy strong enough to resist those feminine charms? Seven thousand dollars came. The raven-haired woman dropped out, sitting down with a look of disgust. But the petite woman was still bidding against the last, unseen bidder.

The whole room was holding its breath as the bidding slowed near the eight-thousand dollar mark. The petite woman was clearly at her breaking point, taking longer and longer to think about each increase. The unseen bidder didn't waver, though. She hit each call without skipping a beat. Jenny scanned the room again, but couldn't see who was pulling the trigger.

Then it was over. The petite bidder couldn't break nine grand. The gavel swung down, and someone else bought Billy. Maybe it was better she didn't know what the winner looked like. That way, it wouldn't haunt her dreams.

One last thing remained, and that was the bike. Ben wheeled it out. Jenny tried to pay attention, because Bobby brought all the kids up on stage, with Seth front and center.

Billy was still out there, looking a little more relieved that the bidding was over. He put his arm around Seth's shoulders as people took photos of them and the bike.

It was hard to look at it. It should have been perfect. Heck, it was perfect. Seth looked up to Billy; Billy had taken her son—a boy he didn't have to do a darned thing for—under his wing. Together they'd built a bike, a real, tangible thing that Seth was proud of. She still wouldn't go so far as to say that Billy was father-material—even cleaned up, he projected an air of danger that was unmistakable—but he'd exceeded her every expectation, and then some.

Yes, it was perfect. Except that someone else had her man.

After the photos, the kids were ushered off stage and the bidding began. Billy stood behind the bike, his hands on the handlebars. He tried to smile—clearly Bobby had told him to—but it looked more like a snarl than anything else. Jenny knew she should pay attention—Seth would want to know how much his bike went for. But all she could think was that she needed to leave before she saw who held Billy's winning bid. And after that? She had a phone now. Maybe she could wait a few days and then call Billy. Hopefully, by then, his evening with the winner would be over and she could try to pretend that it had never happened.

God, what a depressing thought.

The bike went for nearly thirty thousand dollars, which was a darned impressive price. The whole evening had probably raised close to seventy-five thousand dollars for the school. She could run TAPS and feed the kids an evening meal and even pay for prenatal care for years on that kind of money—everything she'd ever wanted and probably some things she hadn't even thought of yet. She should be thrilled. She *would* be thrilled, by God.

Starting tomorrow.

Tonight, she needed to suffer her defeat in peace and quiet. She stood to go get the kids when someone grabbed her arm. "Come with me," Cass said in the kind of voice that left little room for disagreement.

"The kids…"

"You're needed at the registration desk."

Cass didn't explain. Maybe there was a problem with one of the girls helping Josey?

Cass cut through the crowd, pulling Jenny along so fast that she struggled to keep her shoes on. Some of the crowd was departing, but many of the women were hanging around in tight clusters, refreshed drinks in their hands. For them, the night wasn't over.

Cass led her past the line of people waiting to pay, right up to the front. Josey was standing behind Livvy as the girl ran credit cards. "Oh, there you are." Josey grabbed a sheet with a receipt stapled to it. "Here." She shoved the paper into Jenny's hands. "And take this."

"What?" Jenny looked down. It was a receipt, all right— for $8,750. And a ponytail holder. She looked at Josey. "Wait, what?"

"Don't worry about Seth. Mom and I have the kids covered. Have fun!"

"What?" Jenny stared at the paper in her hand again. $8,750—that was how much Billy had sold for. What was going on?

Then a hush came over the crowd. Still swamped with confusion, Jenny looked up and saw Billy—the new and improved Billy—coming toward her. His head was lowered, making him look like a bull charging. Straight at her.

All eyes were on Billy and, by extension, on her.

"Ready?" he asked in an extra-gruff voice.

"What?" Even to her own ears, the refrain was getting tired, but she had no idea what was going on.

"You won me, didn't you? It's time for our date." The

corner of his mouth curved up in a victorious smile—so much easier to see without the beard covering it up.

So much hotter, too.

The crowd around them murmured in curiosity. No doubt about it, she and Billy were the center of attention. Out of the corner of her eye, she thought she saw the petite blond glare at her.

But she didn't care. All she could do was look up into Billy's eyes in wonder. "Now?"

"It's after the auction, isn't it?" His grin got a little more wicked as he took a step closer. She felt the power ripple off of him and surround her. Despite the jealous looks, she felt safer near him now than she ever had.

He'd meant that literally? She looked at Josey, who nodded and waved her away. "I've got the kids," she said again.

Stunned, Jenny looked back down at the receipt in her hand. "Paid in full" was stamped on the top, but she sure as heck hadn't fronted the money.

Realization slapped her across the face. "You?"

There could be no mistaking the look of intent on his face, not with that wolfish grin and certainly not with that covetous gleam in his eyes. "Me."

And he guided her toward the door.

Fourteen

Billy led her to his bike in the parking lot, his hand firmly around her waist. Wait—this wasn't his normal bike. The bike that Jenny had seen at the school only had one seat.

This bike? Same black-and-chrome colors, but the handlebars were so low that they looked almost normal. But that wasn't the biggest change. No, the biggest difference between the other bike and this one was the extra seat on the back, complete with a backrest.

"You planned this all along, didn't you?" she heard herself ask.

"I told you we'd have a date after the auction." He spun her around in a tight embrace. "This is after the auction."

"Why didn't you tell me?"

"It was a surprise." Was she imagining things, or did he blush at that? "And we didn't want Bobby to find out."

That she could see. She didn't want Bobby involved with this at all. "Well, I am surprised." The understatement of the year.

He reached up and brushed her hair away from her mostly bare shoulders. His fingers trailed down her arms, setting off a cascade of goose bumps. "You'll get cold," he said as he stepped back and slipped off his jacket.

Jenny felt her breath catch in her throat. She'd seen his chest bare once, and she'd seen him in T-shirts, with and without his leather riding vest, plenty of times. But the wide expanse of his chest barely contained by a crisp button-up shirt took all of her confusion and uncertainty and agony over the auction and blew it away like a bunch of leaves in a fall breeze. The only thing that was left was sheer, knee-shaking desire.

So she hadn't realized he was such a literalist. He'd gone to this much trouble to rig the auction for her—and plunked down almost nine grand to get a night with her? No schools and—she looked around—not a single camera in sight. She had no idea how that was working—it wasn't a far stretch to say there were a hundred cameras here. But she wasn't in front of one.

A small crowd of jealous-looking women were milling around the front door of the building, looking daggers at her. Seth was out there, too, along with Livvy and a few of the other kids. But they were all standing around Sandra and Josey, waving. Even Seth smiled.

"He'll be okay," Billy said, doing that thing where he read her mind. "He's going home with Ben and Josey. Video games all night."

"You thought of everything, then?"

He draped his jacket around her shoulders and she slipped her arms in. She swam in the huge thing, but it was warm and smelled like Billy—faintly of leather and the wind. Then he swept her hair back into a low tail and waited until she'd secured it with the band Josey had given her.

Billy handed her a small helmet. It fit, another sign of how much he'd planned ahead. She hadn't exactly ridden a lot of motorcycles, but now was not the time to chicken out. Taking a deep breath, she looked at the bike, looked at her dress, and did the only thing she could—hiked her dress almost up to her hips and slid one leg over the seat.

A noise that was far too sexy to be a purr but not aggressive enough to be a straight-up growl came from deep in Billy's chest. Without another word, he slid onto the bike in front of her.

"Hold on," he commanded.

She was only too happy to comply. She slid her arms around his chest, loving the way the warmth of his body surrounded her. Then he fired up the bike and rolled slowly out of the parking lot.

She didn't know where they were going. Well, she knew they were probably headed for his house, the one with the fabled pool table, but she had no idea how long she would be on the back of this bike. Billy gunned it and they flew, the wind biting at her bare legs. She pressed herself farther into Billy's body, trying to steal as much of his body heat as she could.

Billy brought the bike to a stop at a red light. He reached back and slid a hand up her bare leg, all the way up under her dress. The feel of his hand on her bare skin—skin already chilled by the night air—had her doing a lot more than just breaking out in goose bumps. She out and out shivered against him.

Then they were off again, going faster this time. The warmth of Billy's back warred with the cold of the wind, and all of it was topped by the building excitement. A whole night with him. A night where she could be selfish and wouldn't have to second-guess herself in the morning.

Oh, she needed this.

She couldn't tell if Billy lived a great distance from the auction site or if time was playing tricks on her. The bike hummed between her legs, driving stark desire up into her body with a relentless pace. They took a couple of corners a little too fast, so she had to grip Billy extra hard to keep her balance.

Eleven years. The number kept repeating itself. Eleven whole years since she'd done something this wild, this crazy. Eleven years since she'd done something for her and her alone. But she wasn't the same girl she'd been back then. She'd never had sex as an adult, with a man as confident, as *capable,* as Billy. It didn't matter how wild his reputation was—she was making a conscious choice to be with him.

She had no idea what she was doing. Really, her life since Billy had rolled into it had been uncharted territory. None of it—not the slow flirtation, not the tension and most certainly not the dance—was something she'd been sure about.

She turned her face into his back. Even with the wind pulling at them, she could still smell the leather that was him. Without letting go, she spread her fingers against his chest, copping a feel of his massive muscles. She couldn't wait to strip the shirt off of him and touch what she'd only seen. She could hold on for a few more minutes, couldn't she?

Those minutes felt long, but finally they slowed. Jenny could see house lights off at great distances, but none were close to the long drive where Billy was pulling up. Before them was a wall of garage doors—three of them—but that's all she could see of the house. The center door opened and they rolled in before the bike came to a stop. Behind them, the garage door shut with a clang.

When Billy kicked out the stand and the bike lurched to the left, Jenny felt herself clawing at his chest to keep her balance.

"I got you," he said, and she heard the amusement in his voice. "Can you stand?"

She nodded, which was silly. He couldn't see her head

bobbing behind him. She got the helmet off and handed it to him. He hung it off the handlebar and waited. Going slow, she swung her leg over. Her dress was at the breaking point, but as she stood, Billy's hand slid up the inside of her leg to above her knee.

Her legs didn't hold, but it wasn't all bad—he twisted and caught her, that wolfish grin on his face as clear as day. "You okay?"

"Better now."

The time of uncertainty was over. She knew exactly what she wanted to happen, and what was going to happen. All that was left was fervently hoping that those two things were the same.

He was still on the bike, but she stepped into him, straddling his left thigh. It wasn't any closer than they'd been snuggled together on the couch, but the tension between them was so tight it almost crackled.

"You shaved," she whispered, running her fingertips over his newly smooth jaw.

His arm around her waist tightened. "You like it?"

"Makes you look respectable."

Billy notched his eyebrow at her and then pushed his leg up. Jenny gasped at the pressure that hit her center. Her whole body still tingled with the vibrations of the bike, but this? This went way past tingling and straight over to a kind of pain that only had her wanting more.

She ground down on him, although she didn't consciously choose to do so. Her body, so desperate for the good old-fashioned release of an orgasm at someone else's hands, suddenly had a mind of its own.

"Only thing is," Billy said in a smug tone, "I'm not that respectable."

How was it possible they were still on the bike? That he was still sitting there, looking ungodly handsome? Because, as his hands skimmed over her very bare thighs and pulled her dress up even farther, she wasn't even sure of her own name anymore.

"Promises, promises," she managed to get out, clutching at his nice white shirt so hard that the wrinkles might never come out.

His hands hit the edge of her panties and paused, exploring. They were a perfectly respectable pair of panties—pale pink with little brown polka dots. The fanciest pair she owned. What if they weren't sexy enough?

He ran his fingers up under the edges—over her backside, up on her hips, then down between her legs. The only thing that stopped him was his own thigh. The one she was riding.

"I promised you one thing." He slid his hands back—back farther, back higher, until he was palming each of her posterior cheeks underneath her panties.

Her mind spun, trying to think through the fog of want and need and desire that was making thinking very, very difficult. What had he said? She needed to remember. Then it came to her.

It would be worth the wait.

"I'm still waiting."

A quick smile flashed across his face, but it was lost underneath a hot look of focus as he pushed her up on his leg, driving the one spot that needed so much more than a little mechanical vibrating.

She gasped again, feeling the pressure from the inside matching the pressure on the outside as he pushed her up, raised his leg and pushed her up again. The friction—oh, the friction that built between them, barely separated by the thin layer of her panties—even if Jenny had wanted to say something else, she couldn't. She didn't have the words. The movements were small, but the dance? The dance between them was worth it *all*.

The whole time, he watched her with that look of intense concentration on his face. "You're so beautiful," he growled at her as the pressure built and built.

His words hit something inside her that vibrated even more than the bike had. "Yeah?"

Then all coherence left her behind when he leaned down, touching his forehead to hers. "The first time I saw you at the wedding? Yeah. Oh, yeah. You were *beautiful.* Just like now."

How she needed to hear that, needed to believe that. And she did.

Something inside her let go and she surrendered to the way he moved her body for her. The orgasm hit her like a car crash in slow motion, leaving her feeling like she'd been knocked flat while at the same time she crumpled onto him, panting. She could feel his fingerprints on her bottom where he was still stroking her. She'd never been so naked while still clothed before.

"No screaming?" He didn't sound disappointed, though. In fact, he sounded downright cheerful. "Guess I'll have to try harder."

Everything that had gone weak with sexual relief tightened up again in anticipation. He wasn't done with her. And, now that she thought of it, she hadn't even gotten started with him.

Then he picked her up—lifted her straight off the ground as he slung his leg over the bike. Her legs wrapped around his waist, but it wasn't because she was in danger of being dropped. No, he held her up as if she weighed next to nothing, all without losing his balance.

She felt the weight of his erection through his trousers, pressing hard against her very center. That was *harder,* all right. And she was going to have to try it. All of it.

Without another word, he carried her into the house. Jenny supposed it was a nice house, but it was dark and she couldn't see much past Billy's face, Billy's lips, Billy's

shirt. She kissed his neck, his jaw, his mouth all while trying to undo the buttons on his shirt. She wanted to do all
her seeing and touching at the same time.

She got about halfway down his shirt, just enough to
give her a peek at the muscles and the tattoos, when he
kicked open a door. The next thing she knew, she was being
set down on something that felt suspiciously like a bed. A
bed with silk sheets. The kind of bed she'd barely allowed
herself to dream of—and now she was here with Billy.

"No pool table?" she asked as he knelt before her and
peeled his jacket from her shoulders.

He threw the jacket to the side, then worked the zipper at
the back of her dress. It had been a long time since anyone
had undressed her, and she lost herself in the sensation of
his fingers slipping down her back. All she could do was
lean her head against his shoulder. When he had the dress
unzipped, he slid his hands underneath the fabric and caressed her bare skin. For once, the danged goose bumps
were banished by the scorching heat of his touch. Suddenly, she was hotter than she could ever remember being.

"You deserve more than a pool table."

"Oh."

At this, he paused and kissed her hard. "We can always
play pool later."

Oh.

He pulled the dress over her head and threw it behind
him. The dress was probably beyond all hope by this time,
but she didn't care.

When the dress was gone, he said, "Where were we,
from last week?" as he ran his hands up and down her back.

She lifted her legs back around his waist and pulled
him closer. The weight of his erection hit her center, and
a whole lot more than a shiver ran through her. As nice as
that little moment in the garage had been—and it had been

quite nice—it wasn't enough. Already, she wanted more. A whole night's worth.

"Right about here."

"Been waiting for this all week," Billy said, his voice so low that Jenny felt it right in her chest. He tangled his fingers in her hair. "Longer."

"Yeah?" But that was all she got out before his mouth took hold of hers.

Jenny wasn't going to let him have all the fun. She wanted to lose herself in his touch, but part of losing herself was touching back. So she kept at the buttons on his shirt, then the belt and his pants.

Her fingers brushed against his erection, and he groaned into her mouth before he pulled back, tilted her head and grazed his teeth down her neck. "You have protection?"

"Yeah." He leaned over to a small nightstand and snagged a condom.

She went to undo her bra—anything to speed up this process was a good thing—but he grabbed her hands. "I want to do that."

He leaned into her, working the clasp. She was loving the lavish, careful attention he was paying her, but she was getting darned tired of waiting. She wanted him inside her *now,* and each moment that didn't happen felt like another year of celibacy.

So she did the only thing she could. She bit his shoulder. Not hard enough to break his skin, but right now she didn't want slow and gentle or even lavish. She wanted rough and hard and Billy. She wanted the man who'd brought her to a shaking orgasm without even getting off his bike. *Now.*

"Woman," he growled and suddenly she was on her back, covered by his massive body. His shirt was open, his pants were half-off, and his boxer-briefs were straining to the point of failure.

He pressed the length of his body against her as his

tongue tangled with hers. She tried to shove his shirt off, but arms and legs and the remaining clothing were all being helplessly tangled. She shifted her hips, bringing her center in line with his erection, but they still had on too much fabric. "I need you—all of you," she told him while trying to hook her foot into the waistband of his pants so she could kick them off.

He stood back, shucking his shirt and his pants in two blissfully quick moments. Then he removed his boxer-briefs, and she saw.

"Wow" was all she could say.

Back when she'd been young and crazy and sleeping around the rez, she'd been sleeping with boys. For the first time, she saw exactly what sleeping with a man looked like. The difference was measureable—in inches.

His grin held nothing but the promise of what was to come next. Then he pulled her panties off. The bra came next, and he rolled on the condom.

Thank goodness, she thought as he climbed back into bed. The weight between her legs was more than heavy—it positively ached. She spread herself as wide as she could for him, but then he did something unexpected. He turned on the light, rolled onto his back and pulled her on top of him.

"I want to watch you."

She swallowed, feeling self-conscious. "Um…"

But he kept running his fingers over her breasts, her hips, her thighs—all places that she worried about, all places that weren't perfect. His fingertips skimmed the low part of her belly that still sported faint stretch marks after all these years. The whole while, his hips were moving under hers. The huge length of him pressed against her, awakening her to all sorts of wonderful feelings—feelings that weren't necessarily new, but weren't familiar, either. Instead of the hard, pressing want that Billy had sparked outside in his garage, this was a slow, almost languid heat—wet and warm and hard.

"Just when I think you can't get any more beautiful," he said as he sighed.

Jenny felt herself relax. "It's been a long time…." A long time since she'd felt pretty—since someone had *thought* she was pretty. She settled, feeling the pressure of him on the outside of her body. It wasn't enough—this slow, sensual pace. She raised herself and felt him spring up. Then, slowly, she let herself fall onto him.

He filled her and more, but she was able to take him in. Once she'd completely settled, she paused, savoring the feeling. She needed this, needed him, but she didn't want the frenzied, jackrabbit sex she'd had so long ago. She was in bed with a man. She wanted to appreciate the differences.

Billy let her rest, adjusting to his girth while he cupped both of her breasts in his hands. "You feel *good*." His fingers tweaked her nipples, which earned him a small gasp. "You like that?"

She nodded, biting her lip. So he did it again. Harder.

This time, the jolt hit her so hard that she had to rise and fall. Suddenly, he sat up in bed and took her left nipple in his mouth. "Don't stop, woman," he groaned against her skin. Then he scraped his teeth over her flesh and rolled her nipple between his teeth and his tongue and tweaked the other nipple with his hand and she was riding him. Oh, how she was riding him.

She'd wanted him, wanted to dance with him, since that first afternoon in the shop—the first time she'd seen that there was something underneath the scowl and the leather, something deeper, something good.

Billy's hands slipped down her backside as he licked her other nipple. His hands traced where he'd held her against him earlier, then he was pushing her again—up, down, back, forth—pushing her higher and higher. Her breath caught, then he dragged his teeth against her again.

As the climax unleashed itself on her, she cried out, *"Billy!"*

Suddenly he thrust harder and harder, taking her almost to the breaking point before he let out a low roar and fell back onto the bed. His hands didn't leave her, though. Instead, they kept right on stroking her back, her legs, her waist—he traced every inch of her body as she pulled herself free and collapsed next to him.

"Like I told you," Billy said, sounding breathless. It gave her a good feeling—she'd made him just as breathless as he'd made her. "I'm not that respectable."

Jenny pushed herself up and looked him in the eye. "Respectability," she whispered, stretching out against his body and loving the way his arm automatically went around her waist, "is overrated."

Fifteen

Jenny went to get cleaned up and Billy took care of the condom. Man, he thought to himself over and over. He'd been afraid that, after the weeks-long buildup, sex with Jenny wouldn't live up to the expectation. He'd never been more wrong.

He straightened out the sheets and got the pillows lined up. As great as that had been, he'd only had her home for about forty-five minutes. He still had her for the whole night. And a long morning.

Almost nine grand. He had no idea who Josey had been bidding against—but it had been someone who'd been freaking serious about it. Bobby hadn't thought he'd go for much more than four or five, tops. But almost nine? Yeah—he was keeping Jenny here for as long as he wanted.

As long as *she* wanted, that was. Already, he was hardening thinking about the way her warm wetness had taken him in, the way she'd moaned and then cried out his name. The way she'd looked, her breasts bouncing up and down with each thrust.

He shook his head, checking to see if it was on straight. She'd said it herself—it'd been a long time. Even though she'd been able to handle him, she would probably need more than ten minutes of recovery time.

But the image of all her curves wouldn't be banished. Would twenty minutes be enough?

To distract himself, he hung up his jacket and tried to shake out her dress. The thing was a crumpled mess, though. Then the bathroom door opened and he spun to see her backlit with the bathroom light. The sight of her, nude, in his room had him hard all over again. Man, she was so much more than he'd hoped. For such a small woman, she packed a hell of a punch.

"I think your dress is ruined," he said, trying to think about anything but the way the light shined between her legs as she walked over to him, making the V of hair covering her sex glow like a sunset. Didn't work. "I'll buy you another one."

"Can't think of anywhere I'd wear it." Her voice had that low, teasing tone that made his brain misfire.

"I'll take you someplace fancy."

The dress fell to the ground, forgotten again. "You look amazing," he managed to get out. And she did. As sweet as she looked when she was being a teacher and as glamorous as she'd looked tonight, nothing beat her in all of her glorious, nude beauty.

At this, her playfulness took a more anxious turn and she tried to cross her arms in front of those amazing breasts, only to appear to change her mind and try to cover up her lower parts.

"No, don't." He closed the distance between them and took her wrists in his hands. "Don't hide from me."

She was such a little thing—barely came up to his chest. Which was where she was looking now, right at the rose over his heart. When she pulled her hand away, he let her. "If we're not hiding, is this the part where I get to see your tattoos?" Her fingers traced the outline of the rose.

Billy swallowed. Sure, people knew he had tattoos—hard not to. People knew he had this tattoo, in fact. But no one knew what this tattoo represented, what all of them meant. Men—including his brothers—didn't ask. They just said, "Nice tats, man!" and left it at that. A few women had asked over the years but Billy had never wanted to tell those women what his skin meant. So he'd made up crap—the rose was for his mom or whatever sounded good at the time.

This? This was different. He didn't want to lie to her.

So he sucked it up. "Yup."

It was worth it to watch the greedy light in her eyes, worth it when she turned him and pointed him to the bed. "Go."

That's where he wanted her, anyway. Maybe this wouldn't be so bad. Maybe they'd get through the tattoos and get back to more sex real quick.

"Yes, ma'am." And it was totally worth it when she smacked him on the butt.

He sat down on the bed, but she shook her head at him. With her hands on her hips, she looked exactly like she did during daylight hours—scolding and irritated but with that trace of playfulness underneath. "On your stomach, please."

Billy complied, sprawling out on his belly. He felt the bed give under her weight as she climbed over his legs, shivered as her hand skimmed over his butt. She grabbed a handful of cheek and squeezed. She was going to kill him.

Her laugh was light and airy—not afraid of him or his ink. He felt something inside him unclench.

She moved—and suddenly she was straddling him. "No tattoos here?" He could feel each one of her fingertips cutting a path over his butt.

His erection strained against the bed, but it hadn't been

twenty minutes yet, and she wasn't done looking. "I've got a few ideas, but nothing I'm going to drop trou for."

"I see." Then she was running her hands over the swath of black that made up his lower back before it exploded into a tornado of blackbirds that flew free up and over his shoulders. "This is truly impressive, Billy."

"One of a kind." She wasn't just touching him—that would have been torture enough. But she'd scooted up a little, and he could feel the warmth of her body where she was sitting on his backside. All he'd have to do would be to turn over and he could be inside her. The need to do that was so strong that it took him a moment to realize he'd still have to fish a condom out of the nightstand drawer. Damn it. Instead, he fisted the sheets and tried to breathe.

A soft fingertip touched each bird. "What does it mean?"

Billy turned his head so that he could see her out of the corner of his eye. "It's my life. There was a time when I was only this massive tornado of darkness and destruction—I hurt myself, hurt people who cared about me."

"Then you saw the light?" Her weight shifted and he felt her warm breath on his back.

"More like I broke free. Grew up, got smarter, got over it."

Well, gotten *more* over it. He didn't know if he'd ever be all the way over it.

"It's beautiful."

And the funny thing was, she didn't sound like she was jerking his chain. She leaned down far enough that he could feel the weight of those amazing breasts on his back. She kissed one of the birds.

In that moment, Billy not only saw but *felt* the difference between being horny and being something else, something he didn't quite have a name for. Did he want to sink himself into Jenny's sweet body again? Hell, yes. But it wasn't just getting off that pushed him. It was something more—being with Jenny.

It was amazing how much a difference that made.

She slid off of him, which left him colder than he wanted to admit. But she rolled him onto his back—and straddled him again. He couldn't help himself—his hands found her hips and he began to rock back and forth under her—not enough to qualify as sex, but more than enough that she got the message.

She gasped, her eyes widening with what he hoped was pleasure. The feeling of skin on skin—his skin on her skin—was enough to drive all rational thought from his mind. He pulled her down harder, feeling her wetness coat him.

She bit her lip, which probably was a gesture of indecision but happened to look damn sexy. Had it been twenty minutes? Could he get a condom?

"Not yet." She got the words out through gritted teeth as she peeled his hands from her hips.

He had to admire her control, damn it all.

But she didn't scoot off of his erection. She sat there in that narrow space between intimate and not, her chest heaving. Finally, she turned her attention back to his tats. The main one on his chest was a huge skull with black flames on top and a rattlesnake coming out of one eye. The snake went up and over his shoulder.

But next to it was the rose wrapped in thorns. It was the only tattoo he had that was in color. The red was on the edges of the petals, like a tea rose, his mom's favorite flower. It had been the only tattoo of his that she'd ever thought was pretty, even if it was wrapped in thorns.

Billy could see Jenny looking from the big, scary tat to the small, pretty one and he knew that she was smart enough to make more than a few connections.

"So," she began, covering his rose with her palm, "you have a, um, *graphic* tattoo to distract from this one?"

"Yeah." He wanted to cut her off, distract both of them by sliding into her welcoming body—but he couldn't. He had to be honest with her. With himself.

But he couldn't do it with her naked body on top of his. Not when he could look into her eyes. So he squeezed his shut, focusing on the warmth of her hand over his heart.

To his surprise, she slid forward, wrapping her arms around his chest—full-body contact. *Yeah,* he thought, folding her into his arms, *that's better.*

"When I was seventeen, I was dating this girl," he began, not knowing a better place to start. "She was everything I wasn't—smart and pretty with rich parents. I think I was her wild streak—her family hated me. *Hated* me. But she'd sneak out at night."

He felt her head nod against his chest. No doubt, she'd done some of that sneaking out, too. "So what happened?"

"I got her pregnant." Jenny stilled—he didn't think she was even breathing—so he kept going. Stopping and thinking about it sucked more than getting it over with. "And I freaked out. I broke my hand punching a wall, threw a fit—I even broke my bike. Kicked it over. I'd gotten drunk before then, but I went out and got ripping drunk. I…" God, he was so ashamed of what a jerk he'd been. "I couldn't deal with it. Tried to start a fight at this bar I shouldn't have been in, almost got myself killed."

"Is that when you got arrested?"

"Actually, the bartender knew my dad. Called him up. He came and got me, dragged me home and tore me a new one." This part—the part that wasn't his fault—was easier to think of. "He'd gotten my mom pregnant—with me—when they were both eighteen. When I told him what I'd done, he slapped me and told me to get myself together.

Told me I had to marry her—that's what he'd done. Told me that any Bolton baby had to stay a Bolton."

"Did you?"

Billy realized he was stroking her hair. And that she was still here—hadn't bolted because he'd been a huge jerk. Not yet, anyway.

"I slept on it for a few days. Then bought a cheap ring and went to her house to propose."

God, this was hard. He'd only said these things out loud one other time. Not even his brothers knew this. As much of a loudmouth as his father was about some things, Bruce Bolton had kept his mouth shut about this. Billy wasn't even sure if Dad had told Mom before she died. He hoped not, anyway. He wouldn't have wanted her to be so disappointed in him.

He didn't want to disappoint Jenny, either.

"What happened?" Her voice was small—but not scared, not judgmental. She'd been on the other side after all. Maybe she understood being freaked out better than most.

"She said…" His voice caught, and suddenly talking was almost impossible.

Jenny leaned up and kissed him on the cheek before she returned back to her chest-to-chest hug. Then she waited.

"She'd had an abortion. Said she didn't want *it* because she didn't want me—she'd never wanted me. Then she slammed the door in my face."

Jenny gasped in surprise. "She did *what?*"

"Yeah."

They lay there for a few moments. Billy was keenly aware of Jenny—not so much in the sexual sense, but that she was still here in this bed with him, still wrapped up in his arms. That she hadn't called him a filthy, no-good dirtbag who was too stupid to know when he wasn't wanted. All those things that Ashley had said to him.

"I almost got an abortion," Jenny said in her super-quiet voice. "After Ricky left, I wanted it to be over. But my mom wouldn't let me. She said I had to live with what I'd done, and one day I'd thank her for it."

"Did you?"

"Eventually. Like you said, I grew up, got smart and got over it." She traced her fingers over the rose petals. "So, this isn't for the girl."

"No. It's for the baby."

She slid a hand behind his back and caressed the inches of inky blackness that had once been his life. "Then you were lost."

"Yeah." Funny, he didn't feel lost at all right now. More than anything, he felt right—more right than he'd felt in a long time.

"So, what happened?"

He smiled in spite of feeling a little raw. After all that, she was still here, holding him. "I got more and more *gone*. Spent half my days drunk, the other half hungover. Picked fights—earned my nickname, Wild Bill, the hard way. Got arrested a bunch. Then my dad stopped bailing me out. Told me I could rot in jail until I got my head screwed back on. Told me I was killing my mom, the way I was."

He swallowed again. His mom had been so worried about him for so long, no wonder his dad had been furious with him. Mom and Dad might have had to get married, but they'd stuck by each other, through good and bad, until the day the cancer took Mom. After that, Billy hadn't been the only one who was a little lost.

"He left you there?"

"Yup."

"Wow…my mom *just* made me have a baby."

"I wasn't there for years or anything. A couple of months. Then, when my case came up, I had a plea deal. Community service." This was the only part of the story he liked to think about. Coming into the light. "My old shop teacher spoke on my behalf, said he had a plan for how I could talk to the kids in school, kids like me who were lost. He'd make me work it off."

"Your shop teacher stood up for you?"

"Cal Horton. He's the only other person, besides Dad, who knows about this. And you," he added quickly. "So I did work it off. I was twenty-four. I'd lost seven years of my life to drinking and fighting. Cal is pretty much the anti-Dad—wiry little guy, soft-spoken. He'd been the only teacher who didn't write me off in school. The only person who never wrote me off. So he dragged me back to school, made me talk to the kids, made me lead them in picking up an adopted stretch of the highway—and put tools back in my hand. Gave me something to do with my life. After I'd finished with the community service, I went to work for my dad and started building bikes."

Her hand slid up his back, finding the birds again. "Free."

He held her tighter than before. "Free," he agreed.

But lonely. He'd built a hell of a business with his brothers. For ten years, his life had been work. He'd worked on bikes twelve, fourteen hours a day. He'd made a boatload of money, but he hadn't stopped long enough to enjoy it—like enjoying his money took something away from the reason why he did the work. It kept him busy and out of trouble, but hadn't left time for anything else.

Until now. Any other Saturday night, he might be working on his drawings or testing out a new angle for the handlebars—thinking about a bike. Tonight? Tonight he was in bed with a sweet, beautiful woman. And that's damn well where he was going to stay for as long as he could.

"You didn't take the easy way out. You did the right thing, even though it was hard. I want to be good enough for you, Jenny. Because you're so much better than I am."

Her head shot up, nearly clipping him in the chin. She stared at him, her mouth open. He smoothed her hair back from her face before he closed her mouth for her with a kiss. It was true—all of it.

She kissed him back without hesitation, their tongues tangling along with their limbs. *This* was freedom—here, in her arms, being loved by a good woman.

Then she tried to roll him on top of her, but he pulled away. "I like you on top," he said, and put her there.

She frowned at him, even as her hips worked small circles on his aching erection. "Why?"

"Better this way," he got out through gritted teeth. Man, the way she was grinding against him—he leaned over and snagged a condom.

She wasn't having any of that, though. She grabbed the hand holding the condom and pinned it against the bed. "Maybe I want you on top."

"No, you don't." He flexed, knowing good and well that he could break her hold on his hand. But he didn't want to.

Her eyes narrowed. "And why is *that?*"

"Better view."

"Baloney."

Right now—except for the fact that she was naked—she looked exactly like the kind of woman who would threaten to feed him to the coyotes.

"A lot—" No, that wasn't right. He started again. "Other women have complained that I'm too heavy."

The look on her face said, "You can't tell me what to do."

"I'm not afraid of you or your massive, gorgeous chest, Billy." As if to emphasize her point, she rolled off—and pulled him with her.

This wasn't a good idea, but it was clear that she had a point to prove and he wasn't going to get lucky again if he didn't let her prove it. So he rolled into her, pausing only long enough to sit back on his heels and put the condom on. "You tell me if it doesn't work?"

"Absolutely." She reached out and stroked his length, and suddenly, he was ready to go again. "And I'll tell you if it does. Deal?"

"Deal." Then her legs were around his waist, pulling him forward until he hit her wet center.

Billy surrendered himself to the sensations of her body—the way she took him in, the way she surrounded him with her warmth, the way her arms clung to his neck, holding him tight. He stroked into her. It had been so long since he'd been on top that it was like having sex for the first time all over again. Everything about Jenny felt new and different. Any worries he had were blown away with the breathy whispers of how much she liked being with him. Soon, she couldn't even whisper—all she could do was moan his name.

Soon, he couldn't hold anything back. And when her body tightened on his with the force of her orgasm, he lost it all. The release was so intense that, for a moment, everything got a little hazy at the edges. All he could think was of birds flying into the sky, free. That's how he felt with her. Free as a bird.

He pulled away, but he didn't get far. He lay on his side and wrapped his arms around her. Suddenly, he was tired—not the usual stayed-up-all-night-working tired, but something that was infinitely more satisfying.

"Was that okay?" He hoped so, because that was the kind of sex a man could get used to having more of. A lot more of.

Jenny surprised him by giggling. "No." He froze, but she added, "It was *wonderful*."

He exhaled in relief, which became a yawn. "Good."

"Maybe in the morning, we can try a different position."

That was enough to get his eyes open again. "Yeah?"

She kissed him. "Yeah."

Hot damn.

Billy had finally gotten lucky.

Sixteen

Billy hadn't had a lot of spooning sex. But waking up with Jenny in his arms? Yeah, that was the kind of intimate he wanted, with the woman he wanted.

He explored her breasts, her nipples, the space between her legs. And he loved hearing her telling him exactly how good he made her feel, to hear her cry out in pleasure.

But soon enough, they were lying spent and panting, and the morning sun shone bright through the windows. All she had to wear was the crumpled gown, which looked even worse in the light of day. So Jenny walked around in one of his T-shirts while he showed her his place.

"And this is the kitchen, which goes out to the garage." He hoped she liked it—hoped she might want to spend a little more time here with him, but he couldn't tell by the look on her face.

Jenny did a slow circle. "It is always this…empty?"

Billy glanced around, trying to see his house as she did. Everything was in its place—he kept his house like he kept his shop. But he could see her point. He had five bedrooms—and only one bed. His. "Yeah, I guess."

"How long have you lived here?"

"About six years. It's far enough away from the neighbors that they don't complain about engine noise." He got out the eggs and bacon and put the kettle on. Then he set out the four boxes of tea he'd bought for her. "Pick one."

Jenny chose the English breakfast and slid onto the chrome-and-black-leather stool he had at the island counter. "It's a big place."

"You like it? You can come back whenever you want. Seth, too." A strange look crossed her face and she dropped her gaze to the packet of tea in her hands. Maybe she didn't like his big, empty house? "I can get a bed for Seth. He can pick out whatever he'd like."

"I…"

Billy couldn't tell what was worse—the way she wasn't meeting his gaze, or the way her words trailed off. Suddenly, he was on edge.

Last night—this morning—had been amazing for both of them. He'd thought. Had he gotten a woman wrong again—she'd had her one night and that was that? "What?"

"It's just— I don't know— See, I haven't done this for a long time. Eleven years." Her words spilled out of her in a guilty rush. "The last guy I tried to date bailed when Seth started calling him Daddy, and Seth was *crushed*. So I stopped dating. He doesn't remember it, thank goodness. He was only three. But…" As fast as she'd started, she stopped.

Man, eleven years? And his almost-three years had felt like a long time. Then it hit him like a load of bricks. This was like when they'd woken up on Ben's couch last week—practically the first thing out of her mouth was asking Seth what he wanted for breakfast. She was putting herself last, again.

Jenny, the woman, needed some mind-blowing sex and probably had for a long time. But Jenny, the mom, had buried those needs and wants down deep. No wonder she'd had so much energy to unleash on him last night. Eleven years was a hell of a backlog to work through.

She looked up at him, and he was surprised to see tears welling up in her eyes. "I don't know if we should do *that. This.* I have to put his interests first. I mean, you've been wonderful with him, but I don't expect you to suddenly be a father figure to him. And we're so different. I don't have anything and you—you can have everything you want."

"I want you."

She shook her head. "My life is on the rez and your life is in the shop, and I…I don't know how this would work."

He gaped at her for a second, his mind spinning furiously as it tried to come up with the right response. If he were his brother Ben, he'd probably have some logical plan of how, exactly, this would work. If he were Bobby, he'd have the right words to calm her down.

But he wasn't his brothers and never would be. So he did the only thing he could. He walked around the island, took her tear-stained cheeks in his hands, and kissed her. After a few moments, her arms went back around his neck and she held on to him as if she were afraid she might never get the chance to do so again.

"This isn't about the boy, Jenny. He'll be fine. This is about you and me," he told her as he hugged her to his chest.

He felt like a jerk for saying it—for telling her that her own son wasn't important. But he didn't care. He didn't want her sense of duty to pull her away from him.

"I've never known another woman like you—you push me, challenge me—you aren't afraid of me. You make me want to *be* better. I'm not going to let *this* go without a fight because you think your boy might not like it or you think I'm too rich for a woman like you. None of that matters a damn bit to me. I want to be with you, even if it isn't easy."

She looked up at him, her eyes rimmed with red. It hurt

him to see her upset like this, to know he was the reason why. "I have to put my son first."

"Who puts you first?" Maybe he was selfish. Maybe he just wanted to keep her in his bed. But he wasn't going to let guilt ruin this. No way in hell. "That's all I want to do—put you first."

"What will people say if it doesn't work?"

"To hell with them—I don't care." Was she really worried about—what, her reputation? Or was she worried about his? Didn't matter. "If it doesn't work, then it doesn't work. But I know this—I won't regret trying. I'll only regret *not* trying."

She closed her eyes and nodded before breaking out into a watery grin. "No regrets."

He kissed her again. He'd never cared what anyone thought about him.

Until her. She was a good, sweet, thoughtful woman. Maybe she was *too* good for him. Maybe she'd realize that, sooner or later.

He had to show her—he could be good for her. Bacon and eggs and tea—it could all keep. Right now, what he needed was the woman in his arms. He picked her up, pausing only long enough to turn off the kettle.

"None," he told her as he carried her back to bed.

There was no way he could regret this.

No way he could regret *her*.

At first, it wasn't easy. Billy wasn't the kind of guy who liked to talk on the phone, so their conversations were mostly about when they could see each other again.

But in person, he was a different man. From the moment Jenny saw him until the unavoidable moment they parted, Jenny felt like she was the center of his world. She hadn't agreed to spending another night at Billy's house with Seth in tow, but they'd had a few dates. She'd left Seth with her mom and driven into the city. He'd bought her a new dress—a luscious red number with a little shawl—and taken her to the theater to see *Annie Get Your Gun*. He'd worn his suit again and had even made reservations at a super-fancy restaurant.

He was spoiling her. She let him do it. No one had ever spoiled her before.

He'd also come out to the rez and met Jenny's mom. That time, he'd taken her on a wind-whipped ride. They'd had sex on a blanket out in the middle of nowhere. Jenny had been on top for that one. The memory still made her smile.

Bobby had gotten his television deal and, as a result, was no longer filming the webisodes while the show was in preproduction. Jenny didn't know much about it—only that Billy wasn't on camera all day long and that made him happy. And Billy happy was an extremely good thing.

As far as she could tell, Seth was okay with her seeing Billy. They hadn't really talked about it much, so when Seth asked, "Are you and Billy going to get married?" one morning on the drive into school, he totally took her by surprise.

"I don't know," she admitted. There was still a lot to work around.

The drive between her house and his was almost an hour and a half, but she wasn't going to give up her job at the school to move in with him. She couldn't leave her mom, who was getting older, her students or her TAPS girls. She couldn't push all of those people aside because being with Billy made her happier than she could ever remember being.

And that was the other problem. She was starting to think it wasn't just happiness. She was starting to think it might be love.

"Not anytime soon," she added. That, at least, was 100 percent true.

"Would he be my dad?"

Now how was she supposed to answer that? So she hedged. "Sweetie, we'll cross that bridge when we come to it."

It wasn't like Billy was replacing some dearly departed father. But he and Seth were, well, *bonding* in a way that even she couldn't turn a blind eye to. A couple of times, she and Seth had driven in to the Crazy Horse Choppers shop on the weekend, where Billy and Seth worked on designing a new bike together—one that would be for Seth when he turned sixteen. Then Seth would go hang out with Ben and Josey while Billy and Jenny had dinner or played pool or had hot—if quick—sex.

It worked, sort of. Seth got to hang out with Billy, who kept on him about his grades, then Jenny got Billy to herself for a while. He kept asking her to come home with him for the weekend—with Seth in tow. She hadn't said yes yet, but she was thinking about it more and more. He was good with Seth in the shop, but Seth around the house was another thing entirely. Part of her couldn't help but wonder what would happen when Seth left the bathroom trashed and the water running, or what would happen when she and Seth got into one of their usual fights about homework. Would Billy decide he'd had enough?

She wanted to think that wouldn't happen, but she knew there were limits to Seth's star behavior. Sooner or later, it might come down to Seth or Billy.

She was falling for Billy.

But her son had to come first.

She'd cross that bridge when she came to it.

Billy was excited. This was the first Saturday that Jenny had agreed to come spend the night with him—and she was bringing Seth. If things kept moving in this direction, it might not be that much longer before she wanted to stay with him all the time. Permanently.

Because he was thinking about something permanent. He wasn't getting any younger and after finding a new kind of freedom in Jenny's arms, he sure as hell didn't want to go back to being lonely.

Everything was better now. His old man didn't bug him as much. Now that Bobby had his big production deal, he was spending more time in New York and there were no cameras on Billy, so that was a huge victory. It made it a hell of a lot easier to have Jenny meet him at the shop after school and have a date. He discovered he liked dating—taking Jenny out and making her feel special. He had the money. He'd never felt comfortable spending it on himself, but spending it on Jenny? Seeing the way her face lit up when she'd unwrapped the red dress alone had been worth the price tag.

Even work was smoother. Ben had hired some new guys and a full-time salesman. The bikes were selling, but they were meeting their production schedule. Billy had to admit, Bobby's plan to make Crazy Horse Choppers a national brand was working.

He didn't know if Jenny was what made it all work, but she made it all worth it. Recently, Billy had found himself looking at property halfway between the shop and the school—a place where they could meet in the middle. He wasn't married to his house, after all.

But the problem was, he wasn't at the point where he wanted to buy a house for her—and her kid. Because a woman like Jenny wouldn't want to shack up with the likes of him, not without a ring. And he wasn't sure he was the marrying kind. Getting married was something responsible grown-ups did. Sure, he ran a successful company and, yeah, he paid his bills but...wasn't he still the same guy who'd hit bars and got thrown into the drunk tank until he sobered up?

Wasn't he?

Lost in this train of thought, the door to the shop opened and Lance, the new salesman, stuck his head in. "There's a woman here to see you, Mr. Bolton. I mean, Billy."

"She can come on back," he said without looking up from the schematics of Seth's bike. The kid wanted something low and sleek that wasn't a crotch rocket. And it had to be something that Jenny would actually let him ride. Needless to say, they were still in the designing phase.

The first thing he noticed was that the sound wasn't right. Instead of Seth and Jenny talking about school, all he heard was the clicking of heels on concrete. Jenny didn't wear heels if she could help it.

The scent was the second thing. Suddenly, the shop was filled with a heavy floral perfume that clung to his nose.

But the final tip-off was the voice. "You've done well for yourself, Billy," a throaty woman's voice cooed.

It was probably supposed to sound seductive, but Billy heard a distinctive hard edge underneath. The hair on the back of his neck bristled.

Not Jenny. But there was still a chance this was a customer, so he vowed to keep things polite. Moving slowly, Billy pivoted on his stool. Standing about six feet away was a petite woman with big blond hair and huge heels who looked vaguely familiar. "Thanks," he said, purposefully keeping it short. "Can I help you?"

The woman's eyes narrowed even as she smiled and shifted her weight on those heels. She looked as though she were waiting for him to say something. Well, she could keep on waiting. Finally, she said, "You don't remember me." The hard edge in her voice got more distinctive.

The way she stuck a hand on her hip and jutted out her chest… "You were at the bachelor auction, right?"

That was a hell of a vicious smile. "You never were terribly bright, but I thought you'd remember *me*."

Was this some sort of psycho-fan who'd seen all those

webisodes and thought she "knew" him? And what sort of woman walked into his business and accused him of being dumb?

Not a very smart one, that much he knew. "We don't give tours. If you want to buy a bike, Lance is the salesman on duty." He pointed through the door.

"You really don't remember me."

She sounded like a broken record, as if repeating the same thing over and over would help. "No clue, lady."

"And after all we went through in high school."

Everything stopped—breathing, thinking—*everything.* "Ashley?"

No, no, *no.* This was not happening. He prayed to God that he'd gone momentarily insane and was having the worst hallucination ever, because even insanity would be preferable to seeing this woman again.

When he said her name, Ashley's features softened. "You *do* remember."

Like he'd forget the woman who ripped his heart out of his still-beating chest.

"You look different." Which was true enough.

"Better, I hope. And you! You filled out. Quite the tank now, aren't you?"

Had he ever been in love with this woman? Because the woman standing in front of him barely matched up with the girl he remembered. Short, yes—and still curvy. But nothing else seemed right. Hair, face, clothes—all different.

But her dismissive attitude toward him—was that so far off from the girl who'd slammed the door in his face? No. Same person, damn it all.

"What do you want?"

"You're quite famous now, you know that? I've seen all the episodes of your little show. And now you're going to have your own cable TV show? Very impressive, Billy."

He didn't like the way she said his name, and he really

didn't like the tone of her voice. All it did was make one thing painfully clear—she wanted *something,* and it sure as hell wasn't him.

He needed to get her out of here, fast. If Jenny came in—and Ashley recognized her as the woman he'd taken home from the auction—things could get ugly.

"Why are you here?"

"We were good together once, remember?" She preened. Probably trying to look sexy, but he wasn't falling for that. "We had a lot of fun back in high school."

"I was young and stupid then. What do you want?"

That wasn't the right thing to say. Anything friendly or fake about her disappeared, and he found himself looking at a viper in a woman's body. "Do you know that every time I have to fill out all those doctor forms, I have to put down that I had an abortion? Every single time."

"I didn't want you to get the abortion. You did that without asking me. Without even *telling* me."

"You weren't the pregnant one," she snapped back, looking frustrated. "I was the one who was scared and hurting and I'm the one who had to live with it."

"It was my kid, too." Too late, he realized he'd put his hand over his rose tattoo. "You took that away from me."

"And be stuck with you for the rest of my life?" She looked mad enough to spit bullets, but then everything about her changed again and he supposed she was trying to look warm and inviting. It didn't work. "I never thought you'd make it this far, that's for damn sure. If I had, well…" She pivoted and took in the shop. "I'm impressed. Truly."

This was about money, he realized. She saw that he had some and felt entitled to a share, all because he'd gotten her pregnant a long time ago. "How much?"

She smirked. "Never were one to beat around the bush, were you? Although I do recall you punching some walls."

"How much? That's what you want, isn't it?" He'd figured her out. She wanted a payoff or she'd tell everyone what she'd done seventeen years ago—but she'd make it sound like his fault.

He didn't like that smile, not one bit—because it said that he'd hit the nail on the head. "I didn't want it to go like this. I tried to buy you at that auction, see if we could rekindle the spark."

"See if you could get on the show."

She wiped a manicured finger down the side of her mouth, as if she'd tasted something spoiled. "Look at you, catching on so quickly. Maybe I didn't give you enough credit."

"How much to never see you again?" Because right now, that's what he wanted more than anything else in the world.

"Fine. Have it your way. Fifty thousand dollars."

His mouth fell open. So this was what blackmail felt like. This was exactly why he was never comfortable with money in the first place—as soon as you had some, people came out of the woodwork, looking for ways to take their cut.

He never should have let Bobby put him in front of a camera.

She waved her hand around. "Come on—what's the problem? Some of your bikes go for more than thirty thousand. Just build a couple more and sell them."

"It doesn't work like that. All that money is tied up—locked up tight." Hell, if he were able to start cutting checks for fifty grand, he'd have just written one to Jenny's school.

Disappointment flashed over her face, but it was buried beneath a predatory glare. "I wanted to keep this between us, Billy. I tried to buy you with every last dollar I had. I didn't want it to come to this. But I need the money." For a quick moment, she looked scared—and tired. But then it was gone. "And if you won't give it to me, well, there are other people who'll pay for a good scoop."

He needed Bobby here to negotiate—because that's what this was, a negotiation. But he was on his own. "You wouldn't."

"I would. Oh, not right away—I'd let the show get started, let you get more exposure—then the online gossip sites of the world would be willing to fork over a pretty penny for the whole story. Think of the headline—Biker Reality Star Abandoned Pregnant Teen Girlfriend." She waved her hands in front of her face as if she were seeing the title in lights. "I've heard that the head of your new cable network is a real stickler for conservative values. It'd be a damn shame to get your new show canceled after only a few episodes."

A part of him was tempted to let her go right ahead and do that—get it over with. But he knew that, even if the show got canceled, it wouldn't be the end of it. Tabloid stories fed on other tabloid stories. The show would go away, but he'd never have a moment's peace.

Ashley said as much. "Just think—once they get their claws in you? How many women have you slept with, Billy? How many of them would share all the details to get their picture in a magazine? I'm doing you a favor here—offering you a clean break with none of the photographers hiding out in your bushes."

He knew she was right. He also knew that later, he was going to punch Bobby. If his brother hadn't put Billy on camera, none of this would have happened.

Ashley must have interpreted his silence as disagreement. "*You* got me pregnant, Billy." The hard edges melted and she looked ten—no, seventeen—years younger. "*You* freaked out, punched a wall and disappeared for *days*. What was I supposed to do? I was scared, and my parents…well, they never trusted me again. Mom sends me birthday cards, but we don't really talk." She cleared her throat, and Billy could tell she was on the verge of tears.

"So I ended it. I had to. And I couldn't stand to face you. I know I said some horrible things, but I was upset and in pain and I...I didn't want to be the reason my dad didn't love me anymore. That meant you had to be."

"You should have trusted me. I would have taken care of you."

She shook her head, blinking hard. "We were *so* young. Couldn't take care of ourselves, much less a baby. I don't want to ruin your life, Billy—not any more than mine's already been ruined. I just need the money, then you'll never have to see me again. I promise," she added, sounding like she meant it.

The guilt was so heavy that Billy felt his shoulders bowing under it. She was right, damn it all. He'd scared her, then left her all alone. If he'd only...well, no amount of what-ifs were going to change the past. He'd been a jerk. If this was how he had to atone for his sins, so be it. Then he could let go of her and the lost baby.

He needed to let go. And then the rest of his life could be for Jenny and the kid she'd kept.

"Okay."

"Really?"

He stood and motioned her back to the waiting room. He didn't have any checks, but Ben did, up in his office. He wanted to get one written and get Ashley out the door before Jenny got here.

Lance was sitting at the desk, looking nervous. "Stay here," Billy told Ashley. "And don't let her talk to anyone," he added. Especially not Jenny.

He took the stairs to Ben's office two at a time and fumbled his key into the lock. Ben had some computer program that generated checks for the guys. When he'd started using this system, he'd walked Billy through it in case Ben couldn't be there to make payroll.

That had been three years ago—and Ben always made it to work on payday.

Frantic, Billy struggled to get the computer on and find the program. The whole process felt like it was taking hours. Finally, he got the program open and typed out Ashley's information. He had to assume her last name was still the same.

Fifty thousand dollars. Ben was going to kill him for taking this out of the company funds. Hell, the whole family was going to take turns beating the hell out of him. He'd pay the company back, of course, but there wouldn't be any way to hide this from them. As long as it stayed in the family, though...

Billy grabbed the check off the printer and headed down the stairs, praying the whole time that he'd been fast enough.

He hadn't.

Seventeen

Ashley was standing where he'd left her. And there, on the other side of the room, were Jenny and Seth. Seth was sitting in a chair, his backpack at his feet. Jenny stood in front of him, her feet spread and arms crossed over that top that looked so good on her. The look on her face made it perfectly clear that she recognized Ashley for what she was—a threat. The two women were staring at each other with undisguised distrust.

"Here." Billy held the check out to Ashley. Before turning to take it, she raised an eyebrow at Jenny.

He could tell by the small smile on her face that whatever honesty he'd gotten out of her a few minutes ago was gone. All the hard edges were back. "I see your taste in women hasn't changed."

Then she stepped toward him and stood on her tiptoes, as if she was going to kiss him goodbye.

"Don't touch me," he demanded, stepping away from her. "You got what you came for. Now go. That's the deal."

"Indeed." She made a show of inspecting the check. "Goodbye, Billy."

He didn't answer her, and after an awkward second,

she forced a wide smile and walked out of the shop, head held high.

No one in the room moved. Jenny's glare followed Ashley all the way out, then swung around and settled on Billy. Seth's gaze darted between the two of them. Even Lance cowered.

Jenny broke the silence. "Get your bag," she said to Seth. "We're leaving."

The kid opened his mouth to say something, but apparently thought better of it. He grabbed his backpack and stood.

"Wait a minute." Billy must have shouted it, because everyone—everyone but Jenny—shrank back. "Lance, you and Seth—outside. Now."

"We're leaving," Jenny repeated with more force. She didn't back down.

"The hell you are." He wasn't playing this battle. He told Lance, "Get," over his shoulder as he advanced on Jenny.

He was ready for Jenny to do something—bolt, take a swing at him—but he wasn't ready for what happened next. Seth stepped in between them.

"Don't you hurt my mom," he growled, sounding impressively dangerous for a kid who probably weighed a hundred pounds sopping wet. He dropped his bag and balled his hands into fists. "I'm warning you, Billy."

Behind him, Lance squeaked.

"I just want to talk to you," Billy said to Jenny over Seth's head. Then he added, "If you think I'd hurt your mom, kid, then you don't know me very well, do you?"

Seth wavered. Billy could see him turning it over. Then he said, "Fine—but you watch yourself."

Hell, at the rate he was going, Billy half expected the boy to threaten to feed him to the coyotes.

Jenny made a noise of displeasure as Seth hefted his bag and headed out with Lance, who looked relieved to be off the hook. Jenny made a move to follow them, but Billy stood in her way. "Wait, babe."

"Don't you *babe* me."

"At least let me explain." Although he wasn't sure how explaining anything would actually help.

"Explain what? I recognized her—she was the one who didn't win you at the auction. Did she come back to make you a better offer?" At this last bit, her voice broke. But the vulnerability didn't last. The fierceness was back in a heartbeat.

There wasn't a good way to say this. Unfortunately, she took his silence all wrong and tried to shove him away from the door.

Of course, she didn't make a lot of headway. He grabbed her hands and put them over his heart. Over the rose. "No, dammit, listen. That was Ashley."

"Oh, she has a name. How nice. I'm very happy for you."

"She was my high school girlfriend."

Suddenly, Jenny got very still. Her fingers curled into the fabric of his shirt. "The one…"

"Yeah." He knew it was a risk—she could still deck him—but he reached out and caressed her cheek. "She walked into the shop—" he glanced over the desk "—half an hour ago."

"What did she want?" This was quieter. Less angry.

"Money."

"For what?"

"Don't know. Said she needed it, or she'd sell her story to the tabloids."

Jenny's eyes shut, but that didn't mask the look of sorrow on her face. "How much did you give her?"

He had the overwhelming urge to pull Jenny deep into his arms and kiss her hard enough that she forgot all about old girlfriends and lost babies and everything he couldn't change about who he was.

But it wasn't going to happen.

"How much?"

"Fifty thousand dollars."

It was a hard thing to watch. Jenny curled into her self. It was harder to feel the weight of her hand push against his rose tattoo as she backed away from him. But the hardest part? Watching the tears slip past her closed eyes and cut a trail down her pale cheeks.

"Every day," she said, her voice quiet and shaky, "I get up and face my mistakes, Billy. I sit across from them at the table and drive them to school and nag them about homework and laundry. And every single day, I make peace with who I am, the choices I've made, what I've done."

When she opened her eyes, Billy knew he was screwed. He felt it deep in his gut—he'd messed up. He wasn't sure what had her so upset—she didn't *want* him in the tabloids, did she? But even the ink on his skin ached.

"I know I've made mistakes. I *know* that," he said.

Her smile was weak—not a thing of happiness, but a thing of pain. It hurt like hell to see it.

"Knowing what your mistakes are and taking responsibility for them are two different things." Her voice caught. "I can't be with a man who won't face his mistakes, Billy. I can't be with someone who's ashamed of who he is, of what he's done. I can't be with someone who thinks he can throw money at a problem and it'll magically make everything all better, because it won't. It won't change who you are or what you've done." Then she leveled the final blow, the one that went straight through him. "And I won't let my son be around someone like that, either. He has to come first. It was a mistake—*my* mistake—to forget that."

That was it. No "Goodbye, Billy," no "call me when you grow up." She wiped the tears from her face, stepped around him and walked out the door.

Just like that, she was gone.

Without shouting, without a fight, he'd lost Jenny. He'd signed the check himself.

And just like that, he was lost.

Seth hadn't said anything other than the heartbreaking, "Did he hurt you, Mom?" when Jenny had walked out of Crazy Horse Choppers crying.

"No, sweetie," she'd said. Not physically, anyway.

She thought she'd been heartbroken when Ricky had abandoned her when she was seven months pregnant. But then, she thought she'd been in love with him, too. And what the heck had a fifteen-year-old girl known about love? Nothing.

Now, though, she knew.

She knew *exactly* what she was walking away from, *exactly* how big the hole in her heart was going to be.

She walked anyway.

How could she have let it get that far? How could she have thrown caution to the wind and followed another bad boy—another boy who wouldn't take responsibility—off the edge of sanity? God, she'd wanted Billy to be different. She'd wanted to believe that underneath his bad-boy exterior, he was a good, decent, *honorable* man. A man she could be with. A man who would be a good example for her son.

Not someone who paid off old girlfriends. Not someone who put his public image above everything else. Not someone who used money like a bandage. No matter how hard she'd fallen for him, she had to put her son first. And she would not teach him that it paid to treat people as commodities, their loyalties to be bought and sold.

In the days that followed, Jenny was possessed with an almost manic energy. She cleaned her classroom from top to bottom. She did her laundry, her mom's laundry and even some of her neighbors' laundry. She scrubbed the floors in her house. She even considered painting the living room.

When that wasn't enough to keep her mind off the way Billy had looked—hollow—she hit the road. She visited every single girl who'd ever come to a TAPS meeting and a few who hadn't. She had all this great funding now, after all. Time to rededicate herself to the group. Those girls needed her.

Josey called, but Jenny didn't feel like talking on the phone Billy had bought her, so she let it go to voice mail. Eventually, the battery died and Jenny stopped charging it. She put the phone in a drawer.

Seth would go to college in four years. Until that time, she needed to focus on being a parent—to him, to the TAPS girls, to her students. That's who she was. That's what she did.

Four years.

That's at least how long it would take her to get over Billy.

In the weeks since his life had spun out of control, Billy had done nothing *but* think about Jenny. Didn't matter what he was doing—explaining to his family why he'd cut a check that big to a woman no one else remembered, drinking in a bar or getting speeding tickets for driving nowhere way too fast—Jenny was with him. Her tear-streaked face haunted him, awake or asleep.

The fallout could have been worse, he guessed. His father had cussed him out and demanded he pay the company back. Because Ben had his money so locked up, Billy had been forced to ask Bobby to sell off a few bikes from his private collection to make up the difference. To the twerp's credit, he'd not only done it, but he'd done it without a camera crew present.

Worse, though, was that Ben had told Josey. Billy was

sure that Jenny had told her cousin that she and Billy were done, but he didn't know if Jenny had told Josey everything. Either way, Josey knew and wasn't exactly looking at Billy anymore. It was as if he didn't exist.

Billy couldn't go home. The whole place made him think of Jenny and how much he'd wanted her to be there with him. He couldn't go to Ben's and have Josey not look at him. Bobby was in New York taking meetings, and Billy wasn't about to go to Dad's place. And, as much as he wanted to get drunker than he'd ever been before, he didn't. That's not who he was anymore.

So he worked. Building bikes was the only thing that had saved him before. It was his only hope now. Fourteen-hour days became sixteen-hour days became eighteen-hour days. Cass brought him in food or someone ordered a pizza. He slept in his office, when he slept at all. He got a ton of work done, but he didn't feel any better. Maybe he never would.

Maybe that's what he deserved. Part of him thought that she was wrong—Ashley had deserved something after what he'd put her through. And he *needed* Ashley to keep quiet or it might affect business. But that part, however logical it was, was buried by the realization that Jenny was right. He'd tried to work around a problem by paying Ashley off when the only way to eliminate the problem was to face up to it. The only way to be a better man, the man he wanted to be, was to finally accept the mistakes he'd made. And so what if he'd gotten some bad press and lost a little business? He already had more money than he knew what to do with. It's not like he'd be penniless.

Damn it all.

The days ran together. He was sure weekends happened, but he didn't know when. Someone was always in the shop with him—Ben, Jack Roy, even Bobby rolled in his crotch rocket and tuned it up. Billy got the feeling they were baby-sitting him, but didn't care. He just needed to not think about her.

Which meant she was all he thought about.

He didn't know what day it was, didn't care. He'd screwed up the cut on a tailpipe and, instead of cussing like he used to, he realized he was staring at it, dumbfounded. *Maybe I should take a break,* he realized. But he didn't want to. It was entirely possible he was afraid to, except he wasn't afraid of anything.

Then someone tapped him on the shoulder. Actually, it was more of a punch. Billy turned, expecting to see Cass with food she was going to insist he eat. But it wasn't Cass.

Seth stood before him, looking as mad as he'd ever looked. "Take off your mask," he demanded so loudly that Billy heard him through the earplugs.

"Seth? What are you doing here? How did you get here?" Billy pulled out the plugs and took off his welding mask. "Tell me you didn't steal—"

But that was as far as he got. Seth reared back and punched him with everything he had. It wasn't enough to break Billy's jaw, but it hurt.

The shop came to a screeching halt. Half the guys made a move to grab the kid, but with one look, Billy called them off.

Ben came flying down the stairs. Cass must have called him when Seth rolled in. She now stood in the shop, looking more worried than he'd ever seen her. To make matters worse, his dad had come out of his office and was watching the whole thing from the top of the stairs.

"She said you didn't hurt her, but she lied," Seth spat out, his fists still balled up. "You made her happier than I'd ever seen her. I didn't even know she could be happy like that. Then you *hurt* her."

"Seth—" But he didn't get very far.

"And I thought you liked me. I thought I made you

proud." The kid's voice broke and his eyes started to water. But he didn't stop. "I thought you were so cool. I wanted to be just like you. I wanted you to be my *dad*."

"Seth—" he tried again, although he didn't know if he wanted the kid to stop talking so he wouldn't cry in the middle of the shop—or so that he'd stop making Billy feel like crap.

"No!" Seth yelled. He was crying now, but he kept going. And Billy had no choice but to let him. "I'm not done. I don't want to be anything like you. Mom was right. We were better off without my dad, and we're better off without you." He dug into his pocket and slammed two cell phones down onto the workbench. "If you ever hurt her again, you'll have to answer to me."

Now sobbing, he turned and ran out of the shop, pushing Cass aside.

The shop was silent. No men cursed, no tools whined. The kid hadn't hit him that hard, but Billy had never hurt more. The new guys shuffled their feet, unsure about what was happening. But the older guys, guys like Jack Roy? Billy could see the wary look in their eyes. They were judging him. It was nothing compared to the look of contempt his own father was leveling at him, though. Even at this distance, he could see the disappointment on Dad's face. The same look he'd had all those years ago when he left Billy to rot in a jail cell until he got his head back on straight.

Was this what Jenny had meant—facing his mistakes? She was right. She'd always been right.

And now was the time to start facing them.

Billy dropped his mask and ran after the boy. Sure enough, Seth was climbing back into Jenny's rust bucket of a car. When he saw Billy, he fired up the engine and tried to drive off.

Except he didn't get out of neutral. The engine revved, but the wheels didn't turn. Billy got the driver's side door opened before Seth got it in gear. "Get out of there," he yelled, grabbing Seth's arm and hauling him out.

"No. No! You stay away from us!" He tried to jerk out of Billy's hold, and when that didn't work, he started kicking. Billy took his lumps, but he wasn't about to let a hysterical kid go roaring down the highway. No one needed to die today. "You messed everything up! I hate you—*hate* you!"

Billy gritted his teeth as his shins took the worst of it. The kid pounded on his chest for good measure, repeating, "I hate you," over and over until finally he wore down into racking sobs.

Billy did the only thing he could think of—he hugged the boy. "I am proud of you, Seth," he said, his own voice choking up on him. "You're a good kid, and I wanted to be your dad, too." The funny thing was, it was the truth—even if he hadn't realized it until now.

Seth was so worked up he couldn't do anything but shake his head *no*. He didn't believe Billy.

"Does your mom know where you are?" Seth shook his head no again. That settled it. "I'm taking you home."

Eighteen

"What are we going to do tonight?" Jenny asked the girls. She was up to twenty girls now. Only six of them were pregnant. She took this as a victory. It was the only victory she had these days.

"No drinking, no drugs," they chanted in unison.

"And?" she prompted. There was comfort in the familiar, in the routine.

"Do our homework, go to school tomorrow."

Cyndy didn't say this part, but she smiled. She was still recovering from the delivery of a healthy baby girl that had gone home with a loving family only two hours away. Cyndy was due back at school next week.

"Good job, girls. Remember—call me if you need to. Otherwise—" The sound of boots clomping down the hallway stopped her midsentence. She knew the sound of those boots.

Her stomach plummeted. No—*no*. What on God's green earth was Billy Bolton doing here? He couldn't be here! He couldn't walk in here like he owned the place!

But that was as far as she got before Billy opened the

door to her classroom—and shoved Seth in. Her son's whole face was red and he had an ice pack taped to his hand.

"Seth! What—"

Billy cut her off with a wave of his hand. "Tell her," he said, putting his hand on Seth's shoulder.

Seth didn't say a thing.

"What's going on?" Jenny demanded.

"He's the one who screwed up. He's the one who's got to face the music," Billy said, meeting her gaze.

"Fine thing coming from you," she muttered so quietly that only Billy and Seth could hear her.

Billy grunted, but he kept his hand on Seth's shoulder. "Go on, kid."

"I, uh…" Seth sniffed. Billy gave him a little shove without letting him go. "I took your car and went to Billy's shop and punched him."

She gaped at Seth, looking from his iced hand to Billy's face. She could see where one side was redder than the other. "You did *what?* You told me you were going to be helping Don outside!"

Billy gave him that little shove again. "I told Don I'd be in here with you." Billy cleared his throat. "I'm sorry I lied."

The wash of emotions that swamped her was so strong it made her knees wobble. Her son—driving down the highway in her rust bucket of a car? Punching Billy in the face? "Are you all right? Are you hurt?"

Seth swiped at his dripping nose with his unbandaged hand, but he didn't answer. Jenny got the feeling he was too afraid of crying in front of the girls—all of whom were paying rapt attention to the little soap opera playing out in front of them.

"Cass said she didn't think it was broken," Billy said. "She's patched me and my dad up enough after fights—she knows what she's talking about."

Jenny's mouth opened and shut. "Um, good? I guess?"

"Doesn't hurt that much." Seth tried to sound tough, but she could tell how upset he was.

Now, anyway. How upset had he been about the whole thing to take her car and drive the forty-five minutes into Billy's shop to punch down the bigger man? She'd failed— again. She'd been so focused on distracting herself from Billy that she hadn't noticed how much Seth had been bothered by suddenly losing Billy as a mentor—and a friend.

Billy stood there, hand on her son's shoulder, giving her the look that probably scared every other person—including the girls in this room—but she recognized it as the mask he used to hide his nerves.

Aside from the slight swelling where Seth had hit him, he looked good. His beard had grown out a little and his hair was already getting long enough to brush the back of his shirt. But he was still wearing the heavy leathers he wore when he was working.

She didn't want him here, didn't want to face this particular mistake with such an audience.

"I'll deal with you when I get home," she told Seth, pulling him away from Billy's grasp. "Thank you for bringing him back."

Billy notched an eyebrow at her. "I'm not done," he said, sounding serious. "I messed up, too. And I've got to pay the price."

Then he did the weirdest thing. He pulled her chair around to the front of the desk and sat down, facing the TAPS girls.

"Hi, girls," he said, trying to sound friendly but still sounding scary.

She was rooted to her spot. All she could do was watch and listen.

"Jenny's a good teacher, isn't she?" The girls all giggled—they called her Ms. Wawasuck—but they nodded.

"I've learned a lot from her," Billy went on. "I learned I have to face my mistakes."

"Billy—" she said, but then stopped. She didn't know what else to say.

"I know some of you are in here because you made a mistake. And some of you don't want to make the same mistake." Some of the girls were blushing, some were looking at the floor—but no one said a thing. "I want to tell you that I understand—I made the same mistake. I was seventeen when I got a girl pregnant."

A low sound—like a gasp that everyone was trying to keep inside—went through the room. Even Seth tensed next to her. But Billy went on.

"I freaked out. Told the girl I didn't want the baby, didn't want to be a dad. I didn't stand by her when she needed me. I bet some of you have had that happen, too."

Cyndy, sitting in the back, nodded, tears dripping down her face. Jenny realized she was nodding, too.

"I went back and asked her to marry me, but she'd already had an abortion. I told myself that was her mistake—not mine. I blamed her for taking a part of me away—but I never took responsibility for what happened. I—" He paused, his voice breaking.

There was no denying what he was doing—everything she'd asked him to.

When he spoke again, he sounded more vulnerable than she'd ever heard him sound before. "I saw her again a few weeks ago, and she's never made peace with what she did. And the truth is I'd never really faced what I'd done, either." His voice softened. "The truth is we both made mistakes. It takes two people to get pregnant. You can try to put the blame on him, but you have to deal with your part of the situation, too." He looked over his shoulder at Jenny, his eyes shining. "That's what you did," he said to her. "You accepted your part in it and raised a damn fine boy who'd put it all on the line to protect you. But I didn't. And you were right—I've been ashamed of that ever since."

She wouldn't have thought it possible, but as she listened to him, Jenny's heart broke all over again. This wasn't him hiding from the past or trying to bury it under piles of money or guilt. This was him laying it all on the line.

He turned his attention back to the girls. "You may think that we're a bunch of dumb boys—and maybe we all are—but we're just as scared as you are. The only difference is that we can walk away. And some guys do. That's what they have to live with. Make the choices you can live with. That means not having sex, or using condoms. That also means keeping the baby, or giving it up, or whatever. But whatever it is, you have to be able to get up every day of your life and look in the mirror and know you did the best you could."

The silence was profound. No one moved until the younger girls began squirming.

Jenny took a deep breath, hoping she could keep it together. "Okay, that's enough for today. I'll see everyone tomorrow."

She didn't have to say it twice. The room cleared in a matter of moments.

"You, too, kid," Billy said. When Seth didn't start walking, he added, "I gave you my word, remember?"

"Okay." Still holding his iced hand, Seth followed everyone else out.

It was just the two of them. Moving slowly, Billy stood and rolled the chair back under her desk. Then he came up to her.

Jenny wanted to back away from him, tell him that she'd feed him to the coyotes if he touched her—but she couldn't. She couldn't even move as he reached out for her, pulled her into the arms she'd missed so much, and kissed her.

She forgot what she wanted and what she didn't want

and whatever mistake had led her away from this man, because all she could think—all she could feel—was how the world had righted itself. God, she'd missed him. No matter how hard she tried, she'd never stop missing him.

He pulled away, but he didn't go far. Instead, crushing her to his massive chest, he said, "I didn't do right by you, Jenny—that was *my* mistake, the one I have to face every day when I look in the mirror. So I tried not looking in the mirror." A sad smile tugged one corner of his lips up. "Didn't work."

"Oh?" She reached up and touched his lips.

"Tried to get lost again—in work, not in beer," he added. "That didn't work, either."

His arms felt so good around her. How had she thought she could live without this? Without *him?*

"Me, too." At this, his smile got a little less sad. "Even painted my living room."

His arms tightened around her. "So I've been thinking that there's only one way to get over you." He let go of her, but before disappointment could sink her, he was on his knees in front of her, both of her hands in his. "If you'll have me, I'll do better—*be* better. For you and your son."

"You—you mean it?"

He nodded. "I won't make any promises about cussing—too set in my ways. He's heard it all, anyway. But he's a good kid. If he wants me as a dad, I'd be proud to have him as a son." He swallowed, and she saw the fear in his eyes. "I'm not perfect. I work too much. I'm grumpy. My family's a pain in the butt. But if you'll have me as a husband, Jenny, I want you as my wife. I love you."

All she could do was gasp in surprise. He'd broken her heart—but he was putting it back together, one word at a time.

"What if it doesn't work?" she heard herself ask.

"I won't regret trying, Jenny. I won't ever regret not giving up on you."

God, how she'd wanted to hear those words, wanted to believe them. How she wanted to say yes. But something held her back—the reason she'd walked away in the first place. "What if that woman comes back and wants more money?"

The blood drained out of his face—except where her son had hit him. The whole situation was unreal. "She won't get anything else out of me. And if she talks to the press, then I'll deal with that. I won't hide anymore. I don't need to. You taught me that." He swallowed again. "Marry me. The family that I want is you and Seth. That's all I need."

"You promise?"

His smile sharpened, making him look hot and wicked and, more than anything, just like the man she loved. "You should know something about me, Jenny. I keep my promises, or I don't make them. And I promise you that I'll do better by you every day for the rest of our lives."

She let out a breath she hadn't known she'd been holding. "Yes," she told him, and was immediately crushed in a gigantic bear hug.

Then the door opened and Seth stuck his head in. "Are you guys done yet?"

Billy grinned down at her. She'd never seen him look happier than he did right then.

"No," he said, brushing his lips over hers. "We're just getting started."

* * * * *

Look for Bobby's story,
EXPECTING A BOLTON BABY,
coming soon from
Sarah M. Anderson and Harlequin Desire.

COMING NEXT MONTH FROM

HARLEQUIN
Desire

Available October 1, 2013

#2257 YULETIDE BABY SURPRISE
Billionaires and Babies • by Catherine Mann

The holiday spirit has professional rivals Mariama and Rowan caring for an abandoned baby—together. But when playing house starts to feel all too real, will they say yes to becoming a family?

#2258 THE LONE STAR CINDERELLA
Texas Cattleman's Club: The Missing Mogul
by Maureen Child

With her boss missing, housekeeper Mia needs a new gig. What she gets is a makeover, a job posing as cattleman Dave Firestone's fiancée— and a chance at a fairy-tale ending?

#2259 A BEAUTY UNCOVERED • *Secrets of Eden*
by Andrea Laurence

When brazen beauty Samantha starts working for beastly CEO Brody Eden, she's determined to tame him. But to capture his heart she must also heal him body and soul....

#2260 A WOLFF AT HEART
The Men of Wolff Mountain • by Janice Maynard

Switched at birth? Pierce Avery must know, so he hires Nicola to uncover the truth—only to find he needs *her*...until she digs up a secret that could tear them apart.

#2261 A COWBOY'S TEMPTATION
Colorado Cattle Barons • by Barbara Dunlop

Rancher-turned-mayor Seth Jacobs wants a railroad in the valley, but a sexy resort owner proves a very tempting roadblock. He'll convince her to relocate...and then he'll have her in his bed.

#2262 COUNTERING HIS CLAIM • by Rachel Bailey

Inheriting *half* a cruise liner is not what hotelier Luke Marlow expected. But to own it all, he'll have to navigate the waters with his new partner— the unsuspecting and sexy on-board doctor.

HDCNM0913

REQUEST YOUR FREE BOOKS!
2 FREE NOVELS PLUS 2 FREE GIFTS!

HARLEQUIN®

Desire

ALWAYS POWERFUL, PASSIONATE AND PROVOCATIVE

YES! Please send me 2 FREE Harlequin Desire® novels and my 2 FREE gifts (gifts are worth about $10). After receiving them, if I don't wish to receive any more books, I can return the shipping statement marked "cancel." If I don't cancel, I will receive 6 brand-new novels every month and be billed just $4.55 per book in the U.S. or $4.99 per book in Canada. That's a savings of at least 13% off the cover price! It's quite a bargain! Shipping and handling is just 50¢ per book in the U.S. and 75¢ per book in Canada.* I understand that accepting the 2 free books and gifts places me under no obligation to buy anything. I can always return a shipment and cancel at any time. Even if I never buy another book, the two free books and gifts are mine to keep forever.

225/326 HDN F4ZC

Name _____ (PLEASE PRINT)

Address _____ Apt. #

City _____ State/Prov. _____ Zip/Postal Code

Signature (if under 18, a parent or guardian must sign)

Mail to the Harlequin® Reader Service:
IN U.S.A.: P.O. Box 1867, Buffalo, NY 14240-1867
IN CANADA: P.O. Box 609, Fort Erie, Ontario L2A 5X3

Want to try two free books from another line?
Call 1-800-873-8635 or visit www.ReaderService.com.

* Terms and prices subject to change without notice. Prices do not include applicable taxes. Sales tax applicable in N.Y. Canadian residents will be charged applicable taxes. Offer not valid in Quebec. This offer is limited to one order per household. Not valid for current subscribers to Harlequin Desire books. All orders subject to credit approval. Credit or debit balances in a customer's account(s) may be offset by any other outstanding balance owed by or to the customer. Please allow 4 to 6 weeks for delivery. Offer available while quantities last.

Your Privacy—The Harlequin® Reader Service is committed to protecting your privacy. Our Privacy Policy is available online at www.ReaderService.com or upon request from the Harlequin Reader Service.

We make a portion of our mailing list available to reputable third parties that offer products we believe may interest you. If you prefer that we not exchange your name with third parties, or if you wish to clarify or modify your communication preferences, please visit us at www.ReaderService.com/consumerschoice or write to us at Harlequin Reader Service Preference Service, P.O. Box 9062, Buffalo, NY 14269. Include your complete name and address.

HD13R

SPECIAL EXCERPT FROM

 HARLEQUIN®

Desire

What will happen when this beauty tries to tame the beast?

Here's a sneak peek at the next book in
Andrea Laurence's SECRETS OF EDEN *miniseries*,
A BEAUTY UNCOVERED, coming
October 2013 from Harlequin® Desire.

Brody turned on his heel, ready to return to his office and lick his wounds, when she called out to him again.

"Mr. Eden?"

"Yes?" He stopped and faced her.

Sam rounded her desk and approached him. His body tensed involuntarily as she came closer. She reached up to the scarred side of his face, causing his lungs to seize in his chest. What was she doing?

"Your shirt…" Her voice drifted off.

He felt her fingertips gently brush the puckered skin along his neck before straightening his shirt collar. The innocent touch sent a jolt of heat through his body. It was so simple, so unplanned, and yet it was the first time a woman had touched his scars.

His foster mother had often kissed and patted his cheek, and nurses had applied medicine and bandages after various reconstructive procedures, but this was different. As a shiver ran down his spine, it *felt* different, as well.

Without thinking, he brought his hand up to grasp hers. Sam gasped softly at his sudden movement, but she didn't pull away when his scarred fingers wrapped around her own. He was glad. He wasn't ready to let go. His every nerve lit up with awareness, and he was pretty certain she felt it, too. Her dark brown eyes were wide as she looked at him, her moist lips parted seductively and begging for his kiss.

He slowly drew her hand down, his eyes locked on hers. Sam swallowed hard and let her arm fall to her side when he finally let her go. "Much better," she said, gesturing to his collar with a nervous smile. She held up the flash drive in her other hand. "I'll get this printed for you, sir."

"Call me Brody," he said, finding his voice when the air finally moved in his lungs again. He might still be her boss, but suddenly he didn't want any formalities between them. He wanted her to say his name. He wanted to reach out and touch her again. But he wouldn't.

Don't miss
A BEAUTY UNCOVERED by Andrea Laurence,
part of the Secrets of Eden miniseries, available
October 2013 from Harlequin® Desire.

HDEXP0913